Jessie Fothergill

The First Violin

A Novel: Vol. I.

Jessie Fothergill

The First Violin
A Novel: Vol. I.

ISBN/EAN: 9783337044053

Printed in Europe, USA, Canada, Australia, Japan

Cover: Foto ©Andreas Hilbeck / pixelio.de

More available books at **www.hansebooks.com**

A Novel.

"Entbehren follſt du : follſt entbehren!"

IN THREE VOLUMES.

VOL. I.

LONDON :

RICHARD BENTLEY AND SON,

Publishers in Ordinary to her Majesty the Queen.

1878.

To

A. C. H.,

IN SLIGHT TOKEN

OF

MY GRATITUDE AND AFFECTION.

CONTENTS OF VOL. I.

BOOK I.

RES ANGUSTA DOMI.

BOOK II.

LIFE.

CONTENTS.

BOOK III.

EUGEN COURVOISIER.

THE FIRST VIOLIN.

BOOK I.

RES ANGUSTA DOMI.

CHAPTER I.

MISS HALLAM.

"WONDERFUL weather for April!"
Yes, it certainly was wonderful.
I fully agreed with the senti-
ment expressed at different periods of the
day by different members of my family;
but I did not follow their example and
seek enjoyment out of doors—pleasure in
that balmy spring air. Trouble—the first
trouble of my life—had laid her hand heavily
upon me. The world felt disjointed and all

upside-down ; I very helpless and lonely in
it. I had two sisters, I had a father and a
mother ; but none the less was I unable to
share my grief with any one of them ; nay,
it had been an absolute relief to me when
first one and then another of them had left
the house, on business or pleasure intent, and
I, after watching my father go down the
garden-walk, and seeing the gate close after
him, knew that, save for Jane, our domestic,
who was carolling lustily to herself in the
kitchen regions, I was alone in the house.

I was in the drawing-room. Once secure
of solitude, I put down the sewing with
which I had been pretending to employ myself, and went to the window—a pleasant,
sunny bay. In that window stood a small
work-table, with a flower-pot upon it, containing a lilac primula. I remember it distinctly to this day, and I am likely to carry
the recollection with me so long as I live. I
leaned my elbows upon this table, and gazed
across the fields, green with spring grass,
tenderly lighted by an April sun, to where
the river—the Skern—shone with a pleasant,
homely, silvery glitter, twining through the

smiling meadows till he bent round the
solemn overhanging cliff crowned with mournful firs, which went by the name of the
Rifted or Riven Scaur.

In some such delightful mead might the
white-armed Nausicaa have tossed her cow-
slip balls amongst the other maids ; perhaps
by some such river might Persephone have
paused to gather the daffodil—" the fateful
flower beside the rill." Light clouds flitted
across the sky, a waft of wind danced in at
the open window, ruffling my hair mockingly,
and bearing with it the deep sound of a
church-clock striking four.

As if the striking of the hour had been a
signal for the breaking of a spell, the silence
that had prevailed came to an end. Wheels
came rolling along the road up to the door,
which, however, was at the other side of the
house. " A visitor for my father, no doubt,"
I thought indifferently ; " and he has gone
out to read the funeral service for a dead
parishioner. How strange ! I wonder how
clergymen and doctors can ever get accustomed to the grim contrasts amidst which
they live !"

I suffered my thoughts to wander off in some such track as this, but they were all through dominated by a heavy sense of oppression—the threatening hand of a calamity which I feared was about to overtake me, and I had again forgotten the outside world.

The door was opened. Jane held it open and said nothing (a trifling habit of hers, which used to cause me much annoyance), and a tall woman walked slowly into the room. I rose and looked earnestly at her, surprised and somewhat nervous when I saw who she was—Miss Hallam, of Hallam Grange, our near neighbour, but a great stranger to us nevertheless, so far, that is, as personal intercourse went.

"Your servant told me that every one was out except Miss May," she remarked in a harsh, decided voice, as she looked not so much at me as towards me, and I perceived that there was something strange about her eyes.

"Yes ; I am sorry," I began doubtfully.

She had sallow, strongly-marked, but proud and aristocratic features, and a manner

with more than a tinge of imperiousness.
Her face, her figure, her voice were familiar,
yet strange to me—familiar because I had
heard of her, and been in the habit of occasionally seeing her from my very earliest child-
hood ; strange, because she was reserved and
not given to seeking her neighbours' houses for
purposes either of gossip or hospitality. I was
aware that about once in two years she made
a call at our house, the Vicarage, whether as
a mark of politeness to us, or to show that,
though she never entered a church, she still
chose to lend her countenance and approval
to the Establishment, or whether merely out
of old use and habit, I knew not. I only
knew that she came, and that until now it
had never fallen to my lot to be present upon
any of those momentous occasions.

Feeling it a little hard that my coveted
solitude should thus be interrupted, and not
quite knowing what to say to her, I sat
down, and there was a moment's pause.

" Is your mother well ?" she inquired.

" Yes, thank you, very well. She has
gone with my sister to Darton."

" Your father ?"

"He is well too, thank you. He has a funeral this afternoon."

"I think you have two sisters, have you not?"

"Yes; Adelaide and Stella."

"And which are you?"

"May. I am the second one."

All her questions were put in an almost severe tone, and not as if she took very much interest in me or mine. I felt my timidity increase, and yet—I liked her. Yes, I felt most distinctly that I liked her.

"May," she remarked meditatively; "May Wedderburn. Are you aware that you have a very pretty north-country sounding name?"

"I have not thought about it."

"How old are you?"

"I am a little over seventeen."

"Ah! And what do you do all day?"

"Oh!" I began doubtfully, "not much, I am afraid, that is useful or valuable."

"You are young enough yet. Don't begin to do things with a purpose for some time to come. Be happy whilst you can."

"I am not at all happy," I replied, not thinking of what I was saying, and then feeling that I could have bitten my tongue out with vexation. What could it possibly matter to Miss Hallam whether I were happy or not? She was asking me all these questions to pass the time, and in order to talk about *something* while she sat in our house.

"What makes you unhappy? Are your sisters disagreeable?"

"Oh *no!*"

"Are your parents unkind?"

"*Unkind!*" I echoed, thinking what a very extraordinary woman she was, and wondering what kind of experience hers could have been in the past.

"Then I can not imagine what cause for unhappiness you can have," she said composedly.

I made no answer. I repented me of having uttered the words, and Miss Hallam went on:

"I should advise you to forget that there is such a thing as unhappiness. You will soon succeed."

"Yes—I will try," said I in a low voice, as the cause of *my* unhappiness rose up, gaunt,

grim and forbidding, with thin lips curved in a
mocking smile, and glittering, snake-like eyes
fixed upon my face.   I shivered faintly; and
she, though looking quickly at me, seemed to
think she had said enough about my unhappiness.   Her next question surprised me much.

"Are you fair in complexion?" she inquired.

"Yes," said I.   "I am very fair—fairer
than either of my sisters.   But are you near-
sighted?"

"Near sight*less*," she replied, with a bitter
little laugh.   "Cataract.   I have so many
joys in my life that Providence has thought
fit to temper the sunshine of my lot.   I am to
content myself with the store of pleasant re-
membrances with which my mind is crowded,
when I can see nothing outside.   A delightful
arrangement.   It is what pious people call a
'cross' or a 'visitation' or something of that
kind.   I am not pious, and I call it the
destruction of what little happiness I had."

"Oh, I am very, *very* sorry for you," I
answered, feeling what I spoke, for it had
always been my idea of misery to be blind—
shut away from the sunlight upon the fields,

from the hue of the river, from all that "lust
of the eye" which meets us on every side.

"But are you quite alone?" I continued.
"Have you no one to——"

I stopped: I was about to add, "to be
kind to you—to take care of you?" but I
suddenly remembered that it would not do
for me to ask such questions.

"No, I live quite alone," said she abruptly.
"Did you think of offering to relieve my
solitude?"

I felt myself burning with a hot blush all
over my face, as I stammered out :

"I am sure I never thought of anything so
impertinent, but—but—if there was anything
I *could* do—read, or——"

I stopped again. Never very confident in
myself, I felt a miserable sense that I might
have been going too far. I wished most
ardently that my mother or Adelaide had
been there to take the weight of such a conversation from my shoulders. What was my
surprise to hear Miss Hallam say, in a tone
quite smooth, polished, and polite :

"Come and drink tea with me to-morrow
afternoon—afternoon tea I mean. You can

go away again as soon as you like. Will
you ?"

"Oh, thank you. Yes, I will."

"Very well. I shall expect you between
four and five. Good-afternoon."

"Let me come with you to your carriage,"
said I hastily. "Jane—our servant is so
clumsy."

I preceded her with care, saw her seated
in her carriage and driven away towards the
Grange, which was but a few hundred yards
from our own gates, and then I returned to
the house. And as I went in again, my
companion-shadow glided once more to my
side, with soft, insinuating, irresistible impor-
tunity, and I knew that it would be my
faithful attendant for—who could say how
long ?

CHAPTER II.

"Traversons gravement ce méchant mascarade qu'on appelle le monde."

THE houses in Skernford—the houses of the "gentry" that is to say—lay almost all on one side an old-fashioned, sleepy-looking "green," towards which their entrances lay; but their real front, their pleasantest aspect, was on their other side, facing the river which ran below, and down to which their gardens sloped in terraces. Our house, the Vicarage, lay nearest the church; Miss Hallam's house, the Grange, farthest from the church. Between these, larger and more imposing, in grounds beside which ours seemed to dwindle down to a few flower-beds, lay Deeplish Hall, whose owner,

Sir Peter Le Marchant had lately come to
live there, at least for a time.

It was many years since Sir Peter Le
Marchant, whose image at this time was
fated to enter so largely and so much against
my will into all my calculations, had lived at,
or even visited his estate at Skernford. He
was a man of immense property, and report
said that Deeplish Hall, which we innocent
villagers looked upon as such an imposing
mansion, was but one, and not the grandest
of his several country houses. All that I
knew of his history—or rather, all that I had
heard of it, whether truly or not, I was in
no position to say—was but a vague and
misty account ; yet that little had given me a
dislike to him before I ever met him.

Miss Hallam, our neighbour, who lived in
such solitude and retirement, was credited
with having a history—if report had only
been able to fix upon what it was. She was
popularly supposed to be of a grim and
decidedly eccentric disposition. Eccentric
she was, as I afterwards found—as I thought
when I first saw her. She seldom appeared
either in church or upon any other public

occasion, and was said to be the deadly enemy
of Sir Peter Le Marchant and all pertaining
to him. There was some old, far-back
romance connected with it—a romance which
I did not understand, for up to now I had
never known either her or Sir Peter sufficiently
to take any interest in the story, but the report ran that in days gone by—how far gone
by, too, they must have been! Miss Hallam—
a young and handsome heiress, loved very
devotedly her one sister, and that sister—so
much was known as a fact—had become Lady
Le Marchant : was not her monument in the
church between the Deeplish Hall and the
Hallam Grange pews ? Was not the tale of her
virtues and her years—seven and twenty only
did she count of the latter—there recorded ?
That Barbara Hallam had been married to Sir
Peter was matter of history : what was not
matter of history, but of tradition which was
believed in quite as firmly, was that the
Baronet had ill-treated his wife—in what
way was not distinctly specified, but I
have since learnt that it was true ; she
was a gentle creature, and he made her life
miserable unto her. She was idolised by her

elder sister, who, burning with indignation at the treatment to which her darling had been subjected, had become, even in disposition, an altered woman. From a cheerful, open-hearted, generous, somewhat brusque young person, she had grown into a prematurely old, soured, revengeful woman. It was to her that the weak and injured sister had fled; it was in her arms that she had died. Since her sister's death, Miss Hallam had withdrawn entirely from society, cherishing a perpetual grudge against Sir Peter Le Marchant. Whether she had relations or none, friends or acquaintance outside the small village in which she lived, none knew. If so, they limited their intercourse with her to correspondence, for no visitor ever penetrated to her damp old Grange, nor had she ever been known to leave it with the purpose of making any journey abroad. If perfect silence and perfect retirement could hush the tongues of tradition and report, then Miss Hallam's story should have been forgotten. But it was not forgotten. Such things never do become forgotten.

It was only since Sir Peter had appeared

suddenly some six weeks ago at Deeplish Hall, that these dry bones of tradition had for me quickened into something like life, and had acquired a kind of interest for me.

Our father, as Vicar of the parish, had naturally called upon Sir Peter, and as naturally invited him to his house. His visits had begun by his coming to lunch one day, and we had speculated about him a little in advance, half-jestingly, raking up old stories, and attributing to him various evil qualities of a hard and loveless old age. But after he had gone, the verdict of Stella and myself was, "Much worse than we expected." He was *different* from what we had expected. Perhaps that annoyed us. Instead of being able to laugh at him, we found something oppressive, chilling, to me frightful, in the cold sneering smile which seemed perpetually hovering about his thin lips—in the fixed, snaky glitter of his still, intent grey eyes. His face was pale, his manners were polished, but to meet his eye was a thing I hated, and the touch of his hand made me shudder. While speaking in the politest possible manner, he had eyed over Adelaide and me in a manner which I do not think either of us had ever experienced before. I hated him from the moment in which I saw him looking at me with expression of approval. To be approved by Sir Peter Le Marchant, could fate devise anything more horrible ? Yes, I knew now that it could : one might have to submit to the approval, to live in the approval. I had expressed my opinion on the subject with freedom to Adelaide, who to my surprise had not agreed with me, and had told me coldly that I had no business to speak disrespectfully of my father's visitors. I was silenced, but unhappy. From the first moment of seeing Sir Peter, I had felt an uncomfortable, uneasy feeling, which had I been sentimental I might have called a presentiment, but I was not sentimental. I was a healthy young girl of seventeen, believing in true love, and goodness, and gentleness very earnestly; "fancy free," having read few novels, and heard no gossip —a very baby in many respects. Our home might be a quiet one, a poor one, a dull one —our circle of acquaintance small, our distractions of the most limited description

imaginable, but at least we knew no evil, and
—I speak for Stella and myself—thought
none. Our father and mother were persons
with nothing whatever remarkable about
them. Both had been handsome. My
mother was pretty, my father good-looking,
yet. I loved them both dearly. It had
never entered my head to do otherwise than
love them, but the love which made the star
and the poetry of my quiet and unromantic
life was that I bore to Adelaide, my eldest
sister. I believed in her devotedly, and
accepted her judgment, given in her own
peculiar proud, decided way, upon every
topic on which she chose to express it. She
was one and twenty, and I used to think I
could lay down my life for her.

It was consequently a shock to me to hear
her speak in praise—yes, in *praise* of Sir
Peter Le Marchant. My first impulse was to
distrust my own judgment, but no : I could
not long do so. He *was* repulsive ; he was
stealthy, hard, *cruel*, in appearance. I could
not account for Adelaide's perversity in liking
him, and passed puzzled days and racked my
brain in conjecture as to why when Sir Peter

came, Adelaide should be always at home,
always neat and fresh—not like me. Why
was Adelaide, who found it too much trouble
to join Stella and me in our homely concerts,
always ready to indulge Sir Peter's taste for
music, to entertain him with conversation?—
and she *could* talk. She was unlike me in
that respect. I never had a brilliant gift of
conversation. She was witty about the
things she did know, and never committed
the fatal mistake of pretending to be up in
the things she did not know. These gifts of
mind, these social powers, were always ready
for the edification of Sir Peter. By degrees
the truth forced itself upon me. Some one
said — I overheard it—that "that handsome Miss Wedderburn was undoubtedly
setting her cap at Sir Peter Le Marchant."
Never shall I forget the fury which at
first possessed me, the conviction which
gradually stole over me that it was true.
My sister Adelaide, beautiful, proud, clever
—and I had always thought good—had
distinctly in view the purpose of becoming
Lady Le Marchant. I shed countless tears
over the miserable discovery, and dared not

speak to her of it. But that was not the worst. My horizon darkened. One horrible day I discovered that it was I, and not Adelaide, who had attracted Sir Peter's attentions. It was not a scene, not a set declaration. It was a word in that smooth voice, a glance from that hated and chilling eye, which suddenly aroused me to the truth.

Shuddering, dismayed, I locked the matter up within my own breast, and wished with a longing that sometimes made me quite wretched, that I could quit Skernford, my home, my life, which had lost zest for me, and was become a burden to me. The knowledge that Sir Peter admired me absolutely degraded me in my own eyes. I felt as if I could not hold up my head. I had spoken to no one of what had passed within me, and I trusted it had not been noticed; but all my joy was gone. It was as if I stood helpless while a noisome reptile coiled its folds around me.

To-day, after Miss Hallam's departure, I dropped into my now chronic state of listlessness and sadness. They all came back: my father from the church; my mother and Adelaide from Darton, whither they had been on a shopping expedition ; Stella from a stroll by the river. We had tea, and they dispersed quite cheerfully to their various occupations. I, seeing the gloaming gently and dim falling over the earth, walked out of the house into the garden, and took my way towards the river. I passed an arbour in which Stella and I had loved to sit and watch the stream, and talk and read Miss Austen's novels. Stella was there now, with a well-thumbed copy of "Pride and Prejudice" in her hand.

"Come and sit down, May," she apostrophised me. "Do listen to this about Bingley and Wickham."

"No, thank you," said I abstractedly, and feeling that Stella was not the person to whom I could confide my woe. Indeed, on scanning mentally the list of my acquaintance, I found that there was not *one* in whom I could confide. It gave me a strange sense of loneliness and aloofness, and hardened me more than the reading of a hundred satires on the meannesses of society.

I went along the terrace by the river-side, and looked up to the left—traces of Sir

Peter again. There was the terrace of
Deeplish Hall, which stood on a height just
above a bend in the river. It was a fine old
place. The sheen of the glass-houses caught
the rays of the sun and glanced in them. I'
looked rich, old, and peaceful. I had been
many a time through its gardens, and thought
them beautiful, and wished they belonged to
me. Now I felt that they lay in a manner
at my feet, and my strongest feeling respecting
them was an earnest wish that I might never
see them again.

Thus agreeably meditating, I insensibly
left our own garden and wandered on in the
now quickly falling twilight into a narrow
path leading across a sort of No-Man's-Land
into the demesne of Sir Peter Le Marchant.
In my trouble I scarcely remarked where I
was going, and with my eyes cast upon the
ground was wishing that I could feel again as
I once had felt, when

"I nothing had, and yet enough;"

and was sadly wondering what I could do to
escape from the net in which I felt myself
caught, when a shadow darkened the twilight

in which I stood, and looking up I saw Sir Peter, and heard these words :

"Good-evening, Miss Wedderburn. Are you enjoying a little stroll ?"

By, as it seemed to me, some strange miracle all my inward fears and tremblings vanished. I did not feel afraid of Sir Peter in the least. I felt that here was a crisis. This meeting would show me whether my fears had been groundless, and my own vanity and self-consciousness of unparalleled proportions, or whether I had judged truly, and had good reason for my qualms and anticipations.

It came. The alarm had not been a false one. Sir Peter, after conversing with me for a short time, did, in clear and unmistakable terms, inform me that he loved me, and asked me to marry him.

" I thank you," said I, mastering my impulse to cover my face with my hands, and run shuddering away from him. " I thank you for the honour you offer me, and beg to decline it."

He looked surprised, and still continued to urge me in a manner which roused a deep

inner feeling of indignation within me, for it
seemed to say that he understood me to be
overwhelmed with the honour he proposed
to confer upon me, and humoured my timidity
about accepting it. There was no doubt in
his manner ; not the shadow of a suspicion
that I could be in earnest. There *was* something that turned my heart cold within me—
a cool, sneering tone, which not all his professions of affection could disguise. Since
that time I have heard Sir Peter explicitly
state his conception of the sphere of woman
in the world : it was not an exalted one. He
could not even now quite conceal that while
he *told* me he wished to make me his wife
and the partner of his heart and possessions,
yet he knew that such professions were but
words—that he did not sue for my love (poor
Sir Peter ! I doubt if ever in his long life
he was blessed with even a momentary
glimpse of the divine countenance of pure
Love), but offered to buy my youth, and
such poor beauty as I might have, with his
money and his other worldly advantages.

Sir Peter was a blank, utter sceptic with
regard to the worth of women. He did not

believe in their virtue nor their self-respect; he believed them to be clever actresses, and, taken all in all, the best kind of amusement to be had for money. The kind of opinion was then new to me: the effect of it upon my mind such as might be expected. I was seventeen, and an ardent believer in all things pure and of good report.

Nevertheless, I remained composed, sedate, even courteous to the last—till I had fairly made Sir Peter understand that no earthly power should induce me to marry him; till I had let him see that I fully comprehended the advantages of the position he offered me, and declined them.

" Miss Wedderburn," said he at last—and his voice was as unruffled as my own; had it been more angry I should have feared it less —" do you fear opposition? I do not think your parents would refuse their consent to our union."

I closed my eyes for a moment, and a hand seemed to tighten about my heart. Then I said:

" I speak without reference to my parents. In such a matter I judge for myself."

" Always the same answer ?"

" Always the same, Sir Peter."

" It would be most ungentlemanly to press the subject any further." His eyes were fixed upon me with the same cold, snake-like smile. " I will not be guilty of such a solecism. Your family affections, my dear young lady, are strong, I should suppose. Which— whom do you love best ?"

Surprised at the blunt straightforwardness of the question, as coming from *him*, I replied thoughtlessly, " Oh, my sister Adelaide."

" Indeed ! I should imagine she was in every way worthy the esteem of so disinterested a person as yourself. A different disposition, though—quite. Will you allow me to touch your hand before I retire ?"

Trembling with uneasy forebodings roused by his continual sneering smile, and the peculiar evil light in his eyes, I yet went through with my duty to the end. He took the hand I extended, and raised it to his lips with a low bow.

" Good-evening, Miss Wedderburn."

Faintly returning his valediction, I saw him go away, and then in a dream, a maze, a bewilderment, I too turned slowly away, and walked to the house again. I felt, I knew I had behaved well and discreetly, but I had no confidence whatever that the matter was at an end.

CHAPTER III.

"Lucifer, Star of the Morning! How art thou fallen!"

FOUND myself, without having met any one of my family, in my own room, in the semi-darkness, seated on a chair by my bedside, unnerved, faint, miserable with a misery such as I had never felt before. The window was open, and there came up a faint scent of sweet briar and wall-flowers in soft, balmy gusts, driven into the room by the April night-wind. There rose a moon and flooded the earth with radiance. Then came a sound of footsteps; the door of the next room, that belonging to Adelaide, was opened. I heard her come in, strike a match, and light her candle; the click of the catch as the blind rolled down.

There was a door between her room and mine, and presently she passed it, and bearing a candle in her hand, stood in my presence. My sister was very beautiful, very proud. She was cleverer, stronger, more decided than I, or rather, while she had those qualities very strongly developed, I was almost without them. She always held her head up, and had one of those majestic figures which require no back-boards to teach them uprightness, no master of deportment to instil grace into their movements. Her toilette and mine were not, as may be supposed, of very rich materials or varied character ; but while my things always looked as bad of their kind as they could— fitted badly, sat badly, were creased and crumpled—hers always had a look of freshness ; she wore the merest old black merino as if it were velvet, and a muslin frill like a point-lace collar. There are such people in the world. I have always admired them, envied them, wondered at them from afar : it has never been my fate in the smallest degree to approach or emulate them.

Her pale face, with its perfect outlines,

was just illumined by the candle she held, and the light also caught the crown of massive plaits which she wore around her head. She set the candle down. I sat still and looked at her.

" You are there, May," she remarked.

" Yes," was my subdued response.

" Where have you been all evening ?"

" It does not matter to any one."

" Indeed it does. You were talking to Sir Peter Le Marchant. I saw you meet him from my bedroom window."

" Did you ?"

" Did he propose to you ?" she inquired, with a composure which seemed to me frightful. "Worldly," I thought, was a weak word to apply to her, and I was suffering acutely.

" He did."

" Well, I suppose it would be a little difficult to accept him."

" I did not accept him."

" What ?" she inquired, as if she had not quite caught what I said.

" I refused him," said I, slightly raising my voice.

"What are you telling me?"

"The truth."

"Sir Peter has fif—"

"Don't mention Sir Peter to me again," said I nervously, and feeling as if my heart would break. I had never quarrelled with Adelaide before. No reconciliation afterwards could ever make up for the anguish which I was going through now.

"Just listen to me," she said, bending over me, her lips drawn together. "I ought to have spoken to you before. I don't know whether you have ever given any thought to our position and circumstances. If not, it would be as well that you should do so now. Papa is fifty-five years old, and has three hundred a year. In the course of time he will die, and as his life is not insured, and he has regularly spent every penny of his income—naturally it would have been strange if he hadn't—what is to become of us when he is dead?"

"We can work."

"Work!" said she, with inexpressible scorn. "Work! Pray what can we do in the way of work? What kind of education

have we had ? The village schoolmistress
could make us look very small in the matter
of geography and history. We have not
been trained to work, and, let me tell you,
May, unskilled labour does not pay in these
days."

" I am sure you can do anything, Adelaide, and I will teach singing. I *can*
sing."

" Pooh ! Do you suppose that because you
can take C in alt. you are competent to teach
singing ? You don't know how to sing yourself yet. *Your face is your fortune.* So is
mine my fortune So is Stella's her fortune.
You have enjoyed yourself all your life : you
have had seventeen years of play and amusement, and now you behave like a baby. You
refuse to endure a little discomfort, as the
price of placing yourself and your family for
ever out of the reach of trouble and trial.
Why, if you were Sir Peter's wife, you could
do what you liked with him. I don't say
anything about myself; but oh ! May, I
am ashamed of you, I am ashamed of you !
I thought you had more in you. Is it possible that you are nothing but a romp—

nothing but a vulgar tomboy? Good heaven! If the chance had been mine!"

"What would you have done?" I whispered, subdued for the moment, but obstinate in my heart as ever.

"I am nobody now; no one knows me. But if I had had the chance that you have had to-night, in another year I would have been known and envied by half the women in England. Bah! Circumstances are too disgusting, *too* unkind!"

"Oh! Adelaide, nothing could have made up for being tied to that man," said I in a small voice; "and I am not ambitious."

"Ambitious! You are selfish—downright, grossly, inordinately selfish. Do you suppose no one else ever had to do what they did not like? Why did you not stop to *think*, instead of rushing away from the thing like some unreasoning animal?"

"Adelaide! Sir Peter! To *marry* him!" I implored in tears. "How could I? I should die of shame at the very thought. Who could help seeing that I had sold myself to him?"

"And who would think any the worse of

you ?　And what if they did ?　With fifteen thousand a year you may defy public opinion."

" Oh, don't ! don't !" I cried, covering my face with my hands.　" Adelaide, you will break my heart !"

Burying my face in the bed-quilt, I sobbed irrepressibly.　Adelaide's apparent unconsciousness of, or callousness to, the stabs she was giving me, and the anguish they caused me, almost distracted me.

She loosed my arm, remarking, with bitter vexation :

" I feel as if I could shake you !"

She left the room.　I was left to my meditations.　My head—my heart too—ached distractingly ; my arm was sore where Adelaide had grasped it ; I felt as if she had taken my mind by the shoulders and shaken it roughly.　I fastened both doors of my room, resolving that neither she nor any one else should penetrate to my presence again that night.

What was I to do ?　Where to turn ?　I began now to realise that the *Res domi*, which had always seemed to me so abundant for all occasions, were really *Res angusta,* and that circumstances might occur in which they would be miserably inadequate.

CHAPTER IV.

"Zu Rathe gehen, und vom Rath zur That."

Briefe BEETHOVEN'S.

THERE was surely not much in Miss Hallam to encourage confidences; yet, within half an hour of the time of entering her house, I had told her all that oppressed my heart, and had gained a feeling of greater security than I had yet felt. I was sure that she would befriend me. True, she did not say so. When I told her about Sir Peter Le Marchant's proposal to me, about Adelaide's behaviour; when, in halting and stammering tones, and interrupted by tears, I confessed that I had not spoken to my father or mother upon the subject, and that I was not quite sure of their approval of what I had done, she even laughed a little, but not in what could be called an amused manner. When I had finished my tale, she said :

"If I understand you, the case stands thus : You have refused Sir Peter Le Marchant, but you do not feel at all sure that he will not propose to you again. Is it not so ?"

"Yes," I admitted.

"And you dread and shrink from the idea of a repetition of this business ?"

"I feel as if it would kill me."

"It would not kill you. People are not so easily killed as all that ; but it is highly unfit that you should be subjected to a recurrence of it. I will think about it. Will you have the goodness to read me a page of this book ?"

Much surprised at this very abrupt change of the subject, but not daring to make any observation upon it, I took the book—the current number of a magazine—and read a page to her.

"That will do," said she. "Now, will you read this letter, also aloud ?"

She put a letter into my hand, and I read :

"'DEAR MADAM,

"'In answer to your letter of last week, I write to say that I could find the rooms you require, and that by me you will have many good agreements which would make your stay in Germany pleasanter. My house is a large one in the Alléestrasse. Dr. Mittendorf, the oculist, lives not far from here, and the *Städtische Augenklinik*—that is, the eye hospital—is quite near. The rooms you would have are upstairs—suite of salon and two bedrooms, with room for your maid in another part of the house. I have other boarders here at the time, but you would do as you pleased about mixing with them.

"'With all highest esteem,
"'Your devoted,
"'CLARA STEINMANN.'"

"You don't understand it all, I suppose?" said she, when I had finished.

"No."

"That lady writes from Elberthal. You

have heard of Elberthal on the Rhine, I presume ?"

"Oh yes ! A large town. There used to be a fine picture-gallery there ; but in the war between the——"

"There, thank you ! I studied Guy's Geography myself in my youth. I see you know the place I mean. There is an eye hospital there, and a celebrated oculist— Mittendorf. I am going there. I don't suppose it will be of the least use ; but I am going. Drowning men catch at straws. Well, what else can you do ? You don't read badly."

"I can sing—not very well, but I *can* sing."

"You can sing," said she reflectively. "Just go to the piano and let me hear a specimen. I was once a judge in these matters."

I opened the piano, and sang, as well as I could, an English version of " *Die Lotus-blume.*"

My performance was greeted with silence, which Miss Hallam at length broke, remarking :

" I suppose you have not had much training ?"

" Scarcely any."

" Humph! Well, it is to be had, even if not in Skernford. Would you like some lessons?"

" I should like a good many things that I am not likely ever to have."

" At Elberthal there are all kinds of advantages with regard to those things—music and singing, and so on. Will you come there with me as my companion ?"

I heard, but did not fairly understand. My head was in a whirl. Go to Germany with Miss Hallam ; leave Skernford, Sir Peter, all that had grown so weary to me ; see new places, live with new people ; learn something ! No, I did not grasp it in the least. I made no reply, but sat breathlessly staring.

" But I shall expect you to make yourself useful to me in many ways," proceeded Miss Hallam.

At this touch of reality I began to waken up again.

" Oh, Miss Hallam, is it really true ? Do you think they will let me go ?"

" You haven't answered me yet."

" About being useful? I would do anything you like—anything in the world."

" Do not suppose your life will be all roses,
or you will be woefully disappointed. I do
not go out at all ; my health is bad—so is
my temper very often. I am what people
who never had any trouble are fond of calling
peculiar. Still, if you are in earnest, and
not merely sentimentalising, you will take
your courage in your hands and come with
me."

" Miss Hallam," said I, with tragic earnestness, as I took her hand, " I will come.
I see you half mistrust me ; but if I had to
go to Siberia to get out of Sir Peter's way, I
would go gladly and stay there. I hope I
shall not be very clumsy. They say at home
that I am, very, but I will do my best."

" They call you clumsy at home, do they ?"

" Yes. My sisters are so much cleverer
than I, and can do everything so much better
than I can. I *am* rather stupid, I know."

" Very well, if you like to call yourself so,
do. It is decided that you come with me.
I will see your father about it to-morrow. I

always get my own way when I wish it. I leave in about a week."

I sat with clasped hands, my heart so full that I could not speak. Sadness and gladness struggled hard within me. The idea of getting away from Skernford was almost too delightful ; the remembrance of Adelaide made my heart ache.

CHAPTER V.

"Ade nun ihr Berge, ihr väterlich Haus!
Es treibt in die Ferne mich mächtig hinaus."
VOLKSLIED.

CONSENT was given. Sir Peter was not mentioned to me by my parents, or by Adelaide. The days of that week flew rapidly by.

I was almost afraid to mention my prospects to Adelaide. I feared she would resent my good fortune in going abroad, and that her anger at my having spoiled those other prospects would remain unabated. Moreover a deeper feeling separated me from her now—the knowledge that there lay a great gulf of feeling, sentiment, opinion between us, which nothing could bridge over or do away with. Outwardly we might be amiable and friendly to each other, but confidence, union, was fled for ever. Once again in the future, I was destined, when our respective principles had been tried to the utmost, to have her confidence—to see her heart of hearts; but for the present we were effectually divided. I had mortally offended her, and it was not a case in which I could with decency, even, humble myself to her. Once, however, she mentioned the future.

When the day of our departure had been fixed, and was only two days distant : when I was breathless with hurried repairing of old clothes, and the equally hurried laying in of a small stock of new ones ; while I was contemplating with awe the prospect of a first journey to London, to Ostend, to Brussels, she said to me, as I sat feverishly hemming a frill :

"So, you are going to Germany ?"

"Yes, Adelaide."

"What are you going to do there ?"

"My duty, I hope."

"Charity, my dear, and duty too, begins at

home. I should say you were going away leaving your duty undone."

I was silent, and she went on :

" I suppose you wish to go abroad, May ?"

" You know I always *have* wished to go."

" So do I."

" I wish you were going too," said I timidly.

" Thank you. My views upon the subject are quite different. When *I* go abroad I shall go in a different capacity to that you are going to assume. I will let you know all about it in due time."

" Very well," said I, almost inaudibly, having a vague idea as to what she meant, but determined not to speak about it.

The following day the curtain rose upon the first act of the play—call it drama, comedy, tragedy, what you will—which was to be played in my absence. I had been up the village to the post-office, and was returning, when I saw advancing towards me two figures which I had cause to remember— my sister's queenly height; her white hat over her eyes, and her sunshade in her hand,

and beside her the pale face, with its ragged eyebrows and hateful sneer, of Sir Peter Le Marchant.

Adelaide, not at all embarrassed by his company, was smiling slightly, and her eyes with drooped lids glanced downwards towards the Baronet. I shrank into a cottage to avoid them as they came past, and waited. Adelaide was saying :

" Proud—yes, I am proud, I suppose. Too proud, at least, to——"

There ! Out of hearing. They had passed. I hurried out of the cottage, and home.

The next day I met Miss Hallam and her maid (we three travelled alone) at the station, and soon we were whirling smoothly along our southward way—to York first, then to London, and so out into the world, thought I.

BOOK II.

LIFE.

CHAPTER I.

"Ein Held aus der Fremde, gar kühn."

WE had left Brussels and Belgium behind, had departed from the regions of *Chemins de fer,* and entered those of *Eisenbahnen.* We were at Cologne, where we had to change, and wait half an hour before we could go on to Elberthal. We sat in the *Wartesaal,* and I had committed to my charge two bundles, with strict injunctions not to lose them.

Then the doors were opened, and the people made a mad rush to a train standing somewhere in the dim distance. Merrick, Miss Hallam's maid, had to give her whole and entire attention to her mistress. I followed close in their wake, until, as we had almost come to the train, I cast my eyes downwards and perceived that there was missing from my arm a grey shawl of Miss Hallam's, which had been committed to my charge, and upon which she set a fidgety kind of value, as being particularly warm or particularly soft.

Dismayed, I neither hesitated nor thought, but turned, fought my way through the throng of people to the waiting-room again, hunted every corner, but in vain, for the shawl. Either it was completely lost, or Merrick had, without my observing it, taken it under her own protection. It was not in the waiting-room. Giving up the search I hurried to the door: it was fast. No one more, it would seem, was to be let out that way; I must go round, through the passages into the open hall of the station, and so on to the platform again. More easily said than done. Always, from my earliest youth up, I have had a peculiar faculty for losing myself.

On this eventful day I lost myself. I ran through the passages, came into the great open place surrounded on every side by doors leading to platforms, offices, or booking-offices. Glancing hastily round, I selected that door which appeared to my imperfectly-developed "locality" to promise egress upon the platform, pushed it open, and going along a covered passage, and through another door, found myself, after the loss of a good five minutes, in a lofty, deserted wing of the station, gazing wildly at an empty platform, and feverishly scanning all the long row of doors to my right, in a mad effort to guess which would take me from this delightful *terra incognita* back to my friends.

Gepäck-Expedition, I read, and thought it did not sound promising. *Telegraphs bureau.* Impossible ! *Ausgang.* There was the magic word, and I, not knowing it, stared at it and was none the wiser for its friendly sign. I heard a hollow whistle in the distance. No doubt it was the Elberthal train going away, and my heart sank deep, deep within my breast. I knew no German word. All I could say was "Elberthal;" and my nearest

approach to " first-class " was to point to the
carriage doors and say " *Ein,*" which might
or might not be understood—probably not,
when the universal stupidity of the German
railway official is taken into consideration,
together with his chronic state of gratuitous
suspicion that a bad motive lurks under every
question which is put to him. I heard a
subdued bustle coming from the right hand in
the distance, and I ran hastily to the other
end of the great empty place, seeing, as I
thought, an opening. Vain delusion! Decep-
tive dream of the fancy! There was a glass
window through which I looked and saw a
street thronged with passengers and vehicles.
I hurried back again to find my way to
the entrance of the station and there try
another door, when I heard a bell ring
violently—a loud groaning and shrieking, and
then the sound, as it were, of a train depart-
ing. A porter—at least a person in uniform,
appeared in a doorway. How I rushed up
to him! How I seized his arm, and dropping my rugs gesticulated excitedly and
panted forth the word " Elberthal!"

" Elberthal?" said he in a guttural

bass ; " *Wollt ihr nach Elberthal, Fräulein-chen ?*"

There was an impudent twinkle in his eye, as it were impertinence trying to get the better of beer, and I reiterated " Elberthal," going very red, and cursing all foreign speeches by my gods—a process often employed, I believe, by cleverer persons than I, with reference to things they do not understand.

" *Schon fort, Fräulein,*" he continued, with a grin.

" But where—what—*Elberthal !*"

He was about to make some further reply, when, turning, he seemed to see some one, and assumed a more respectful demeanour. I too turned, and saw at some little distance from us a gentleman sauntering along, who, though coming towards us, did not seem to observe us. Would he understand me if I spoke to him ? Desperate as I was, I felt some timidity about trying it. Never had I felt so miserable, so helpless, so utterly ashamed as I did then. My lips trembled as the new-comer drew nearer, and the porter, taking the opportunity of quitting a scene

which began to bore him, slipped away. I
was left alone on the platform, nervously
snatching short glances at the person slowly,
very slowly approaching me. He did not
look up as if he beheld me or in any way
remarked my presence. His eyes were bent
towards the ground : his fingers drummed a
tune upon his chest. As he approached, I
heard that he was humming something. I
even heard the air : it has been impressed
upon my memory firmly enough since, though
I did not know it then—the air of the March
from Raff's Fifth Symphonie, the "Lenore."
I heard the tune softly hummed in a mellow
voice as, with face burning and glowing, I
placed myself before him. Then he looked
suddenly up, as if startled, fixed upon me a
pair of eyes which gave me a kind of shock ;
so keen, so bright, so commanding were they,
with a kind of tameless freedom in their
glance such as I had never seen before.

Arrested (no doubt by my wild and excited
appearance), he stood still and looked at me,
and as he looked a slight smile began to dawn
upon his lips. Not an Englishman. I should
have known him for an outlander anywhere.

I remarked no details of his appearance; only
that he was tall and had, as it seemed to me, a
commanding bearing. I stood hesitating and
blushing. (To this very day the blood comes
to my face as I think of my agony of blushes
in that immemorial moment.) I saw a handsome—a very handsome face, quite different
from any I had ever seen before : the startling
eyes before spoken of, and which surveyed
me with a look so keen, so cool and so bright,
which seemed to penetrate through and
through me ; while a slight smile curled the
light moustache upwards—a general aspect
which gave me the impression that he was
not only a personage, but a very great personage—with a flavour of something else
permeating it all which puzzled me and made
me feel embarrassed as to how to address
him. While I stood inanely, trying to gather
my senses together, he took off the little cloth
cap he wore, and bowing, asked :

" *Mein Fräulein,* in what can I assist
you ?"

His English was excellent—his bow like
nothing I had seen before. Convinced that
I had met a genuine, thorough fine gentle-

man (in which I was right for *once* in my
life), I began :

"I have lost my way," and my voice
trembled in spite of all my efforts to steady
it. " In the crowd I lost my friends, and—I
was going to Elberthal, and I turned the
wrong way—and—"

" Have come to destruction, *nicht wahr ?*"
He looked at his watch, raised his eyebrows,
and shrugged his shoulders. " The Elberthal
train is already away."

" Gone !" I dropped my rugs and began a
tremulous search for my pocket-handkerchief.
" What *shall* I do ?"

" There is another—let me see—in one
hour—two—*will 'mal nachsehen*. Will you
come with me, Fräulein, and we will see
about the trains."

" If you would show me the platform,"
said I. " Perhaps some of them may still
be there. Oh, what *will* they think of me ?"

" We must go to the *Wartesaal*," said he.
" Then you can look out and see if you see
any of them."

I had no choice but to comply.

My benefactor picked up my two bundles,

and, in spite of my expostulations, carried them with him. He took me through the door inscribed *Ausgang,* and the whole thing seemed so extremely simple now, that my astonishment as to *how* I could have lost myself increased every minute. He went before me to the waiting-room, put my bundles upon one of the sofas, and we went to the door. The platform was almost as empty as the one we had left. I looked round, and though it was only what I had expected, yet my face fell when I saw how utterly and entirely my party had disappeared.

" You see them not ?" he inquired.

" No—they are gone," said I, turning away from the window and choking down a sob, not very effectually. Turning my damp and sorrowful eyes to my companion, I found he was still smiling to himself as if quietly amused at the whole adventure.

" I'll go and see at what time the trains go to Elberthal. Suppose you sit down— yes ?"

Passively obeying, I sat down and turned my situation over in my mind, in which kind of agreeable mental legerdemain I was still occupied when he returned.

"It is now half-past three, and there is a train to Elberthal at seven."

"*Seven !*"

"Seven : a very pleasant time to travel, *nicht wahr?* Then it is still quite light."

"So long! Three hours and a half," I murmured dejectedly, and bit my lips, and hung my head. Then I said, "I am sure I am much obliged to you. If I might ask you a favour ?"

"*Bitte, mein Fräulein !*"

"If you could show me exactly where the train starts from, and—could I get a ticket now, do you think ?"

"I'm afraid not, so long before," he answered, twisting his moustache, as I could not help seeing, to hide a smile.

"Then," said I, with stoic calmness, "I shall never get to Elberthal—*never*, for I don't know a word of German, not one." I sat more firmly down upon the sofa, and tried to contemplate the future with fortitude.

"I can tell you what to say," said he, removing with great deliberation the bundles

which divided us, and sitting down beside
me. He leaned his chin upon his hand and
looked at me, ever, as it seemed to me,
with amusement tempered with kindness,
and I felt like a very little girl indeed.

"You are exceedingly good," I replied,
"but it would be of no use. I am so
frightened of those men in blue coats and
big moustaches. I should not be able to say
a word to any of them."

"German is sometimes not unlike English."

"It is like nothing to me, except a great
mystery."

"*Billet* is 'ticket,'" said he persua-
sively.

"Oh, is it?" said I, with a gleam of hope.
"Perhaps I could remember that. *Billet*," I
repeated reflectively.

"Bil*let*," he amended; "not *Bi*llit."

"Bill-yet—Bill-*yet*," I repeated.

"And 'to Elberthal' may be said in one
word, 'Elberthal.' '*Ein Billet—Elberthal—
erster Classe..*"

"*Ein Bill-yet*," I repeated automatically,
for my thoughts were dwelling more upon

the charming quandary in which I found myself, than upon his half-good-natured, half-mocking instructions : " *Ein Bill-yet, firste—erste*—it is of no use. I can't say it. But "—here a brilliant idea struck me—" if you would write it out for me on a paper, and then I could give it the man : he would surely know what it meant."

" A very interesting idea, but a *vivâ voce* interview is so much better."

" I wonder how long it takes to *walk* to Elberthal !" I suggested darkly.

" Oh, a mere trifle of a walk. You might do it in four or five hours, I dare say."

I bit my lips, trying not to cry.

" Perhaps we might make some other arrangement," he remarked. " I am going to Elberthal too."

" You ? Thank heaven !" was my first remark. Then, as a doubt came over me : " Then why—why—— "

Here I stuck fast, unable to ask why he had said so many tormenting things to me, pretended to teach me German phrases, and so on. The words would not come out. Meanwhile he, without apparently feeling it necessary to explain himself upon these points, went on :

"Yes. I have been at a *Probe*" (not having the faintest idea as to what a *Probe* might be, and not liking to ask, I held my peace and bowed assentingly). He went on, "And I was delayed a little. I had intended to go by the train you have lost, so if you are not afraid to trust yourself to my care we can travel together."

"You—you are very kind."

"Then you are *not* afraid ?"

"I—oh no ! I should like it very much. I mean I am sure it would be very nice."

Feeling that my social powers were as yet in a very undeveloped condition, I subsided into silence, as he went on :

"I hope your friends will not be *very* uneasy ?"

"Oh *dear* no !" I assured him, with a pious conviction that I was speaking the truth.

"We shall arrive at Elberthal about 8.30."

I scarcely heard. I had plunged my hand into my pocket, and found—a hideous conviction crossed my mind. *I had no money !*

I had, until this moment totally forgotten having given my purse to Merrick to keep; and she, as pioneer of the party, naturally had all our tickets under her charge. My heart almost stopped beating. It was unheard of, horrible, this possibility of falling into the power of a total, utter stranger—a foreigner—a—heaven only knew what! Engrossed with this painful and distressing problem, I sat silent, and with eyes gloomily cast down.

"One thing is certain," he remarked. "We do not spend three hours and a half in the station. *I* want some dinner. A four hours' *Probe* is apt to make one a little hungry. Come, we will go and have something to eat."

The idea had evidently come to him as a species of inspiration, and he openly rejoiced in it.

"I am not hungry," said I; but I was, very. I knew it now that the idea "dinner" had made itself conspicuous in my consciousness.

"Perhaps you think not; but you are, all the same," he said. "Come with me,

Fräulein. You have put yourself into my hands ; you must do what I tell you."

I followed him mechanically out of the station and down the street, and I tried to realise that instead of being with Miss Hallam and Merrick, my natural and respectable protectors, safely and conventionally plodding the slow way in the slow continental train to the slow continental town, I was parading about the streets of Köln with a man of whose very existence I had half an hour ago been ignorant; I was dependent, too, upon him, and him alone, for my safe arrival at Elberthal. And I followed him unquestioningly, now and then telling myself, by way of feeble consolation, that he was a gentleman—he certainly was a gentleman—and wishing now and then, or trying to wish, with my usual proper feeling, that it had been some nice old lady with whom I had fallen in : it would have made the whole adventure blameless, and, comparatively speaking, agreeable.

We went along a street, and came to an hotel, a large building, into which my conductor walked, spoke to a waiter, and we

were shown into the restaurant, full of round
tables, and containing some half-dozen parties
of people. I followed, with stony resignation. It was the severest trial of all, this
coming to an hotel alone with a gentleman in
broad daylight. I caught sight of a reflection in a mirror of a tall, pale girl, with
heavy, tumbled auburn hair, a brown hat
which suited her, and a severely simple
travelling-dress. I did not realise until I
had gone past that it was my own reflection
which I had seen.

"Suppose we sit here," said he, going to a
table in a comparatively secluded window
recess, partially overhung with curtains.

"How very kind and considerate of him!"
thought I.

"Would you rather have wine or coffee,
Fräulein?"

Pulled up from the impulse to satisfy my
really keen hunger by the recollection of my
"lack of gold," I answered hastily:

"Nothing, thank you—really nothing."

"Oh, *doch!* You must have something,"
said he, smiling. "I will order something.
Don't trouble about it."

"Don't order anything for me," said I, my cheeks burning again. "I shall not eat anything."

"If you do not eat, you will be ill. Remember, we do not get to Elberthal before eight," said he. "Is it perhaps disagreeable to you to eat in the saal? If you like we can have a private room."

"It is not that at all," I replied; and seeing that he looked surprised, I blurted out the truth. "I have no money. I gave my purse to Miss Hallam's maid to keep, and she has taken it with her."

With a laugh, in which, infectious though it was, I was too wretched to join:

"Is that all? *Kellner!*" cried he.

An obsequious waiter came up, smiled sweetly and meaningly at us, received some orders from my companion, and disappeared.

He seated himself beside me at the little round table.

"He will bring something at once," said he, smiling.

I sat still. I was not happy, and yet I could not feel all the unhappiness which I considered appropriate to the circumstances.

My companion took up a *Kölnische Zeitung,*
and glanced over the advertisements, while I
looked a little stealthily at him, and for the
first time took in more exactly what he was
like, and grew more puzzled with him each
moment. As he leaned upon the table, one
slight, long, brown hand propping his head,
and half lost in the thick, fine brown hair
which waved in large, ample waves over his
head, there was an indescribable grace, ease,
and negligent beauty in the attitude. Move
as he would, let him assume any possible or
impossible attitude, there was still the same
grace, half careless, yet very dignified in the
position he took.

All his lines were lines of beauty, but
beauty which had power and much masculine
strength ; nowhere did it degenerate into
flaccidity, nowhere lose strength in grace.
His hair was long, and I wondered at it.
My small experience in our delightful home
and village circle had not acquainted me with
that flowing style ; the young men of my
acquaintance cropped their hair close to the
scalp, and called it the modern style of hair-
pressing. It had always looked to me more like

hair-undressing. This hair fell in a heavy wave
over his forehead, and he had the habit, common to people whose hair does so, of lifting
his head suddenly and shaking back the
offending lock. His forehead was broad,
open, pleasant, yet grave. Eyes, as I had
seen, very dark, and with lashes and brows
which enhanced the contrast to a complexion
at once fair and pale. A light moustache,
curving almost straight across the face, gave
a smiling expression to lips which were otherwise grave, calm, almost sad. In fact, looking nearer, I thought he did look sad; and
though when he looked at me his eyes were
so piercing, yet in repose they had a certain
distant, abstracted expression, not far removed from absolute mournfulness. Broad-
shouldered, long-armed, with a *physique* in
every respect splendid, he was yet very distinctly removed from the mere handsome
animal which I believe enjoys a distinguished
popularity in the latter-day romance.

Now, as his eyes were cast upon the paper,
I perceived lines upon his forehead, signs
about the mouth and eyes telling of a firm,
not to say imperious disposition; a certain

curve of the lips, and of the full, yet delicate nostril, told of pride both strong and high. He was older than I had thought, his face sparer; there were certain hollows in the cheeks, two lines between the eyebrows, a sharpness, or rather somewhat worn appearance of the features, which told of a mental life, keen and consuming. Altogether, an older, more intellectual, more imposing face than I had at first thought; less that of a young and handsome man, more that of a thinker and student. Lastly, a cool ease, deliberation, and leisureliness about all he said and did, hinted at his being a person in authority, accustomed to give orders and see them obeyed without question. I decided that he was, in our graceful home phrase, "master in his own house."

His clothing was unremarkable—grey summer clothes, such as any gentleman or any shopkeeper might wear; only in scanning him no thought of shopkeeper came into my mind. His cap lay upon the table beside us, one of the little grey *Studentenhüte* with which Elberthal soon made me familiar, but which struck me then as odd and outlandish. I

grew every moment more interested in my
scrutiny of this, to me, fascinating and remarkable face, and had forgotten to try to
look as if I were not looking, when he looked
up suddenly, without warning, with those
bright, formidable eyes, which had already
made me feel somewhat shy as I caught
them fixed upon me.

" *Nun*, have you decided ?" he asked, with
a humorous look in his eyes, which he was
too polite to allow to develop itself into a
smile.

" I—oh, I beg your pardon !"

" You do not want to," he answered, in im-
perfect idiom. " But *have* you decided ?"

" Decided what ?"

" Whether I am to be trusted ?"

" I have not been thinking about that," I
said uncomfortably, when to my relief the
appearance of the waiter with preparations
for a meal saved me further reply.

" What shall we call this meal ?" he asked,
as the waiter disappeared to bring the repast
to the table. " It is too late for the *Mittag-
essen*, and too early for the *Abendbrod*. Can
you suggest a name ?"

" At home it would be just the time for afternoon tea."

" Ah, yes ! Your English afternoon tea is very——" He stopped suddenly.

" Have you been in England ?"

" This is just the time at which we drink our afternoon coffee in Germany," said he, looking at me with his impenetrably bright eyes, just as if he had never heard me. " When the ladies all meet together to talk scan—*Oh, behüte !* what am I saying ?—to consult seriously upon important topics, you know. There are some low-minded persons who call the whole ceremony a *Klatsch*— *Kaffeeklatsch*. I am sure you and I shall talk seriously upon important subjects, so suppose we call this our *Kaffeeklatsch*, although we have no coffee to it."

" Oh yes, if you like."

He put a piece of cutlet upon my plate, and poured yellow wine into my glass. Endeavouring to conduct myself with the dignity of a grown-up person and to show that I did know something, I inquired if the wine were hock.

He smiled. " It is not Hochheimer—not

Rheinwein at all—he—no, it, you say—it is
Moselle wine—' Doctor.'"

"Doctor?"

"*Doctorberger*; I do not know why so
called. And a very good fellow too—so say
all his friends, of whom I am a warm one.
Try him."

I complied with the admonition, and was
able to say that I liked *Doctorberger*. We
ate and drank in silence for some little time,
and I found that I was very hungry. I also
found that I could not conjure up any real
feeling of discomfort or uneasiness, and that
the prospective scolding from Miss Hallam
had no terrors in it for me. Never had I felt
so serene in mind, never more at ease in every
way, than now. I felt that this was wrong—
Bohemian, irregular, and not respectable, and
tried to get up a little unhappiness about
something. The only thing that I could
think of was:

"I am afraid I am taking up your time.
Perhaps you had some business which you
were going to when you met me."

"My business, when I met you, was to
catch the train to Elberthal, which was

already gone, as *you* know. I shall not be able to fulfil my engagements for to-night, so it really does not matter. I am enjoying myself very much."

"I am very glad I did meet you," said I, growing more reassured as I found that my companion, though exceedingly polite and attentive to me, did not ask a question as to my business, my travelling companions, my intended stay or object in Elberthal—that he behaved as a perfect gentleman—one who is a gentleman throughout, in thought as well as in deed. He did not even ask me how it was that my friends had not waited a little for me, though he must have wondered why two people left a young girl, moneyless and ignorant, to find her way after them as well as she could. He took me as he found me, and treated me as if I had been the most distinguished and important of persons. But at my last remark he said, with the same odd smile which took me by surprise every time I saw it:

"The pleasure is certainly not all on your side, *mein Fräulein*. I suppose from that you have decided that I *am* to be trusted?"

I stammered out something to the effect
that " I should be very ungrateful were I not
satisfied with—with such a——" I stopped,
looking at him in some confusion. I saw a
sudden look flash into his eyes and over his
face. It was gone again in a moment—so
fleeting that I had scarce time to mark it, but
it opened up a crowd of strange, new impressions to me, and while I could no more have
said what it was like the moment it was gone,
yet it left two desires almost equally strong in
me—I wished in one and the same moment
that I had for my own peace of mind never
seen him—and that I might never lose sight
of him again : to fly from that look, to remain
and encounter it. The tell-tale mirror in the
corner caught my eye. At home they used
sometimes to call me, partly in mockery,
partly in earnest, "Bonny May." The so-
briquet had hitherto been a mere shadow, a
meaningless thing, to me. I liked to hear it,
but had never paused to consider whether it
were appropriate or not. In my brief intercourse with my venerable suitor, Sir Peter, I
had come a little nearer to being actively
aware that I was good-looking, only to anathe-

matise the fact. Now, catching sight of my
reflection in the mirror, I wondered eagerly
whether I really were fair, and wished I had
some higher authority to think so, than the
casual jokes of my sisters. It did not add to
my presence of mind to find that my involun-
tary glance to the mirror had been intercepted
—perhaps even my motive guessed at—he
appeared to have a frightfully keen instinct.

" Have you seen the Dom ?" was all he
said; but it seemed somehow to give a point
to what had passed.

" The Dom—what is the Dom ?"

" The *Kölner Dom;* the cathedral."

" Oh no ! Oh, should we have time to see
it ?" I exclaimed. " How I *should* like it !"

" Certainly. It is close at hand. Suppose
we go now."

Gladly I rose, as he did. One of my most
ardent desires was about to be fulfilled—not
so properly and correctly as might have been
desired, but—yes, certainly more pleasantly
than under the escort of Miss Hallam, grumb-
ling at every groschen she had to unearth in
payment.

Before we could leave our seclusion there

came up to us a young man who had looked at
us through the door and paused. I had seen
him; had seen how he said something to a
companion, and how the companion shook his
head dissentingly. The first speaker came up
to us, eyed me with a look of curiosity, and
turning to my protector with a benevolent
smile, said :

"Eugen Courvoisier! *Also hatte ich doch
Recht!*"

I caught the name. The rest was of course
lost upon me. Eugen Courvoisier? I liked
it, as I liked him, and in my young enthusiasm decided that it was a very good name.
The new comer, who seemed as if much
pleased with some discovery, and entertained
at the same time, addressed some questions to
Courvoisier, who answered him tranquilly
but in a tone of voice which was very freez-
ing; and then the other, with a few words and
an unbelieving kind of laugh, said something
about a *schöne Geschichte*, and, with another
look at me, went out of the coffee-room again.

We went out of the hotel, up the street to
the cathedral. It was the first cathedral I
had ever been in. The shock and the wonder

of its grandeur took my breath away. When
I had found courage to look round, and up at
those awful vaults the roofs, I could not help
crying a little. The vastness, coolness, still-
ness and splendour crushed me—the great
solemn rays of sunlight coming in slanting
glory through the windows—the huge height
—the impression it gave of greatness, and of a
religious devotion to which we shall never
again attain ; of pure, noble hearts, and
patient, skilful hands, toiling, but in a spirit
that made the toil a holy prayer—carrying
out the builder's thought—great thought
greatly executed—all was too much for me,
the more so in that while I *felt* it all I could
not analyse it. It was a dim, indefinite
wonder. I tried stealthily and in shame to
conceal my tears, looking surreptitiously at
him in fear lest he should be laughing at me
again. But he was not. He held his cap in
his hand—was looking with those strange,
brilliant eyes fixedly towards the high altar,
and there was some expression upon his face
which I could not analyse—not the expression
of a person for whom such a scene has grown
or can grow common by custom—not the ex-

pression of a sight-seer who feels that he must admire ; not my own first astonishment. At least he felt it—the whole grand scene, and I instinctively and instantly felt more at home with him than I had done before.

" Oh !" said I at last, " if one could stay here for ever, what would one grow to ?"

He smiled a little.

" You find it beautiful ?"

" It is the first I have seen. It is much more than beautiful."

" The first you have seen ? Ah, well, I might have guessed that."

" Why ? do I look so countrified ?" I inquired, with real interest, as I let him lead me to a little side-bench, and place himself beside me. I asked in all good faith. About him there seemed such a cosmopolitan ease, that I felt sure he could tell me correctly how I struck other people—if he would.

" Countrified—what is that ?"

" Oh, we say it when people are like me— have never seen anything but their own little village, and never had any adventures, and—"

" Get lost at railway stations, *und so*

weiter. I don't know enough of the meaning of 'countrified' to be able to say if you are so, but it is easy to see that you—have not had much contention with the powers that be."

"Oh, I shall not be stupid long," said I comfortably. "I am not going back home again."

"So!" He did not ask more, but I saw that he listened, and proceeded communicatively:

"Never. I have—not quarrelled with them exactly, but had a disagreement, because—because—"

"Because?"

"They wanted me to—I mean, an old gentleman—no, I mean—"

"An old gentleman wanted you to marry him, and you would not," said he, with an odd twinkle in his eyes.

"Why, how *can* you know?"

"I think, because you told me. But I will forget it if you wish."

"Oh no! It is quite true. Perhaps I *ought* to have married him."

"*Ought!*" He looked startled.

"Yes. Adelaide—my eldest sister—said so. But it was no use. I was very unhappy, and Miss Hallam, who is Sir Peter's deadly enemy—he is the old gentleman, you know—was very kind to me. She invited me to come with her to Germany, and promised to let me have singing lessons."

"Singing lessons?"

I nodded. "Yes; and then when I know a good deal more about singing, I shall go back again and give lessons. I shall support myself, and then no one will have the right to want to make me marry Sir Peter."

"*Du lieber Himmel!*" he ejaculated, half to himself. "Are you very musical, then?"

"I can sing," said I. "Only I want some more training."

"And you will go back all alone and try to give lessons?"

"I shall not only *try*, I shall do it." I corrected him.

"And do you like the prospect?"

"If I can get enough money to live upon, I shall like it very much. It will be better than living at home and being bothered."

" I will tell you what you should do before you begin your career," said he, looking at me with an expression half wondering, half pitying.

" What ? If you could tell me anything."

" Preserve your voice, by all means, and get as much instruction as you can; but change all that waving hair, and make it into unobjectionable smooth bands of no particular colour. Get a mask to wear over your face, which is too expressive; do something to your eyes to alter their—"

The expression then visible in the said eyes seemed to strike him, for he suddenly stopped, and with a slight laugh, said :

" *Ach, was rede ich für dummes Zeug !* Excuse me, *mein Fräulein.*"

" But," I interrupted earnestly, " what do you mean ? Do you think my appearance will be a disadvantage to me ?"

Scarcely had I said the words than I knew how intensely stupid they were, how very much they must appear as if I were openly and impudently fishing for compliments. How grateful I felt when he answered, with a grave directness, which had nothing but the highest compliment in it—that of crediting me with right motives :

"*Mein Fräulein,* how can I tell? It is only that I knew some one, rather older than you, and very beautiful, who had such a pursuit. Her name was Corona Heidelberger, and her story was a sad one."

" Tell it me," I besought.

" Well, no, I think not. But—sometimes I have a little gift of foresight, and that tells me that you will not become what you at present think. You will be much happier and more fortunate."

" I wonder if it would be nice to be a great operatic singer," I speculated.

" *Oh, behüte !* don't think of it !" he exclaimed, starting up and moving restlessly. " You do not know—*you* an opera singer—"

He was interrupted. There suddenly filled the air a sound of deep, heavenly melody, which swept solemnly adown the aisles, and filled with its melodious thunder every corner of the great building. I listened with my face upraised, my lips parted. It was the organ, and presently, after a wonderful melody, which set my heart beating—a

melody full of the most witchingly sweet
high notes, and a breadth and grandeur of
low ones such as only two composers have
ever attained to, a voice—a single woman's
voice—was upraised. She was invisible, and
she sang till the very sunshine seemed
turned to melody, and all the world was
music—the greatest, most glorious of earthly
things.

> " Blute nur, liebes Herz !
>   Ach, ein Kind das du erzogen,
>   Das an deiner Brust gesogen,
>   Drohet den Pfleger zu ermorden
>   Denn es ist zur Schlange worden."

" What is it ?" I asked below my breath,
as it ceased.

He had shaded his face with his hand, but
turned to me as I spoke, a certain half-sup-
pressed enthusiasm in his eyes.

" Be thankful for your first introduction to
German music," said he, " and that it was
grand old Johann Sebastian Bach whom you
heard. That is one of the soprano solos in
the *Passions-musik*—that *is* music."

There was more music. A tenor voice was
singing a recitative now, and that exquisite

accompaniment, with a sort of joyful solemnity, still continued. Every now and then, shrill, high, and clear, penetrated a chorus of boys' voices. I, outer barbarian that I was, barely knew the name of Bach and his *Matthäus Passion*, so in the pauses my companion told me by snatches what it was about. There was not much of it. After a few solos and recitatives, they tried one or two of the choruses. I sat in silence, feeling a new world breaking in glory around me, till that tremendous chorus came; the organ notes swelled out, the tenor voice sang, "Whom will ye that I give unto you?" and the answer came, crashing down in one tremendous clap, "Barrabam!" And such music was in the world, had been sung for years, and I had not heard it. Verily, there may be revelations and things new under the sun every day.

I had forgotten everything outside the cathedral—every person but the one at my side. It was he who roused first, looking at his watch and exclaiming:

"*Herrgott!* We must go to the station, Fräulein, if we wish to catch the train."

And yet I did not think he seemed very
eager to catch it, as we went through the
busy streets in the warmth of evening, for it
was hot, as it sometimes is in pleasant April,
before the withering east winds of the
"merry month" have come to devastate the
land, and sweep sickly people off the face of
the earth. We went slowly through the
moving crowds to the station, into the
Wartesaal, where he left me while he went
to take my ticket. I sat in the same corner
of the same sofa as before, and to this day
I could enumerate every object in that
Wartesaal.

It was after seven o'clock. The outside
sky was still bright, but it was dusk in the
waiting-room and under the shadow of the
station. When "Eugen Courvoisier" came
in again, I did not see his features so distinctly as lately in the cathedral. Again he
sat down beside me, silently this time. I
glanced at his face, and a strange, sharp,
pungent thrill shot through me. The companion of a few hours — was he only
that?

"Are you very tired?" he asked gently,

after a long pause. "I think the train will not be very long now."

Even as he spoke, clang, clang, went the bell, and for the second time that day I went towards the train for Elberthal. This time no wrong turning, no mistake. Courvoisier put me into an empty compartment, and followed me, said something to a guard who went past, of which I could only distinguish the word *allein;* but as no one disturbed our privacy, I concluded that German railway guards, like English ones, are mortal.

After debating within myself for some time, I screwed up my courage and began :

"Mr. Courvoisier—your name is Courvoisier, is it not ?"

"Yes."

"Will you please tell me how much money you have spent for me to-day ?"

"How much money ?" he asked, looking at me with a provoking smile.

The train was rumbling slowly along, the night darkening down. We sat by an open window, and I looked through it at the grey, Dutch-like landscape, the falling dusk, the poplars that seemed sedately marching along with us.

" Why do you want to know how much ?" he demanded.

" Because I shall want to pay you, of course, when I get my purse," said I. " And if you will kindly tell me your address, too—but how much money did you spend ?"

He looked at me, seemed about to laugh off the question, and then said :

" I *believe* it was about three thalers ten groschen, but I am not at all sure. I cannot tell till I do my accounts."

" Oh dear !" said I.

" Suppose I let you know how much it was," he went on, with a gravity which forced conviction upon me.

" Perhaps that would be the best," I agreed. " But I hope you will make out your accounts soon."

" Oh, very soon. And where shall I send my bill to ?"

Feeling as if there were something not *quite* as it should be in the whole proceeding, I looked very earnestly at him, but could find

6—2

nothing but the most perfect gravity in his expression. I repeated my address and name slowly and distinctly, as befitted so business-like a transaction, and he wrote them down in a little book.

"And you will not forget," said I, "to give me your address when you let me know what I owe you."

"Certainly—when I let you know what you owe me," he replied, putting the little book into his pocket again.

"I wonder if any one will come to meet me," I speculated, my mind more at ease in consequence of the business-like demeanour of my companion.

"Possibly," said he, with an ambiguous half smile, which I did not understand.

"Miss Hallam—the lady I came with—is almost blind. Her maid had to look after her, and I suppose that is why they did not wait for me," said I.

"It must have been a very strong reason, at any rate," he said gravely.

Now the train rolled into the Elberthal station. There were lights, movement, a storm of people all gabbling away in a foreign tongue. I looked out. No face of any one I knew. Courvoisier sprang down and helped me out.

"Now I will put you into a *Droschke*," said he, leading the way to where they stood outside the station.

"Alléestrasse, thirty-nine," he said to the man.

"Stop one moment," cried I, leaning eagerly out. At that moment a tall, dark girl passed us, going slowly towards the gates. She almost paused as she saw us. She was looking at my companion; I did not see her face, and was only conscious of her as coming between me and him, and so annoying me.

"Please let me thank you," I continued. "You have been so kind, so very kind—"

"Oh, *bitte sehr!* It was so kind in you to get lost exactly when and where you did," said he, smiling. "*Adieu, mein Fräulein*," he added, making a sign to the coachman, who drove off.

I saw him no more. "Eugen Courvoisier" —I kept repeating the name to myself, as if I were in the very least danger of forgetting it—" Eugen Courvoisier."— Now that I had parted from him I was quite clear as to my own feelings. I would have given all I was worth—not much, truly—to see him for one moment again.

Along a lighted street with houses on one side, a gleaming shine of water on the other, and trees on both, down a cross way, then into another street, very wide, and gaily lighted, in the midst of which was an avenue.

We stopped with a rattle before a house door, and I read, by the light of the lamp that hung over it, " 39."

CHAPTER II.

ANNA SARTORIUS.

WAS expected. That was very evident. An excited - looking *Dienstmädchen* opened the door, and on seeing me, greeted me as if I had been an old friend. I was presently rescued by Merrick, also looking agitated.

"Ho, Miss Wedderburn, at last you are here! How Miss Hallam *have* worried, to be sure."

"I could not help it, I'm very sorry," said I, following her upstairs—up a great many flights of stairs, as it seemed to me, till she ushered me into a sitting-room, where I found Miss Hallam.

"Thank heaven, child! you are here at

last. I was beginning to think that if you did not come by this train, I must send some one to Köln to look after you."

"By *this* train!" I repeated blankly. "Miss Hallam—what—do you mean? There has been no other train."

"Two: there was one at four and one at six. I cannot tell you how uneasy I have been at your non-appearance."

"Then—then—" I stammered, growing hot all over. "Oh, how *horrible!*"

"What is horrible?" she demanded. "And you must be starving. Merrick, go and see about something to eat for Miss Wedderburn. Now," she added as her maid left the room, "tell me what you have been doing."

I told her everything, concealing nothing.

"Most annoying!" she remarked. "A gentleman, you say. My dear child, no gentleman would have done anything of the kind. I am very sorry for it all."

"Miss Hallam," I implored, almost in tears, "please do not tell any one what has happened to me. I will never be such a fool again. I know now—and you may trust me. But *do* not let any one know how—*stupid* I **have** been.

I told you I was stupid—I told you several times. I am sure you must remember."

" Oh yes, I remember. We will say no more about it."

" And the grey shawl," said I.

" Merrick had it."

I lifted my hands and shrugged my shoulders. " Just my luck," I murmured resignedly, as Merrick came in with a tray.

Miss Hallam, I noticed, continued to regard me now and then as I ate with but small appetite. I was too excited by what had passed, and by what I had just heard, to be hungry. I thought it kind, merciful, humane in her to promise to keep my secret and not expose my ignorance and stupidity to strangers.

" It is evident," she remarked, " that you must at once begin to learn German, and then if you do get lost at a railway station again, you will be able to ask your way."

Merrick shook her head with an inexpressibly bitter smile.

" I'd defy any one to learn *this* 'ere language, ma'am. They call an accident a *Unglück:* if any one could tell me what *that* means, I'd thank them, that's all."

"Don't express your opinions, Merrick, unless you wish to seem deficient in understanding ; but go and see that Miss Wedderburn has everything she wants—or rather everything that can be *got*—in her room. She is tired, and shall go to bed."

I was only too glad to comply with this mandate, but it was long ere I slept. I kept hearing the organ in the cathedral, and that voice of the invisible singer—seeing the face beside me, and hearing the words, "Then you have decided that I *am* to be trusted ?"

"And he was deceiving me all the time !" I thought mournfully.

I breakfasted by myself the following morning, in a room called the *Speisesaal.* I found I was late. When I came into the room, about nine o'clock, there was no one but myself to be seen. There was a long table with a white cloth upon it, and rows of the thickest cups and saucers it had ever been my fate to see, with distinct evidences that the chief part of the company had already breakfasted. Baskets full of *Brödchen* and

pots of butter, a long indiarubber pipe coming
from the gas to light a *Theemaschine*—lots of
cane-bottomed chairs, an open piano, two
cages with canaries in them; the kettle gently
simmering above the gas-flame ; for the rest,
silence and solitude.

I sat down, having found a clean cup and
plate, and glanced timidly at the *Theemaschine,*
not daring to cope with its mysteries, until
my doubts were relieved by the entrance of a
young person with a trim little figure, a
coquettishly cut and elaborately braided apron,
and a white frilled *Morgenhaube* upon her
hair, surmounting her round, heavenward-
aspiring visage.

" *Guten morgen, Fräulein,*" she said, as she
marched up to the darkly mysterious *Theemaschine* and began deftly to prepare coffee
for me, and to push the *Brödchen* towards
me. She began to talk to me in broken
English, which was very pretty, and while I
ate and drank, she industriously scraped little
white roots at the same table. She told me
she was Clara, the niece of Frau Steinmann,
and that she was very glad to see me, but was
very sorry I had had so long to wait in Köln,

yesterday. She liked my dress, and was it *echt Englisch*—also, how much did it cost?

She was a cheery little person, and I liked her. She seemed to like me too, and repeatedly said she was glad I had come. She liked dancing, she said. Did I? And she had lately danced at a ball with some one who danced so well—*aber*, quite indescribably well. His name was Karl Linders, and he was, ach! really a remarkable person. A bright blush, and a little sigh, accompanied the remark. Our eyes met, and from that moment Clara and I were very good friends.

I went upstairs again, and found that Miss Hallam proposed, during the forenoon, to go and find the Eye Hospital, where she was to see the oculist, and arrange for him to visit her, and shortly after eleven we set out.

The street that I had so dimly seen the night before, showed itself by daylight to be a fair, broad way. Down the middle, after the pleasant fashion of continental towns, was a broad walk, planted with two double-rows of linden, and on either side this Lindenallée was the carriage road, private houses, shops, exhibitions, boarding-houses.

In the middle, exactly opposite our dwelling,
was the New Theatre, just drawing to the
close of its first season. I looked at it without thinking much about it. I had never
been in a theatre in my life, and the name
was but a name to me.

Turning off from the pretty allée, and from
the green *Hofgarten* which bounded it at
one end, we entered a narrow, ill-paved street,
the aspect of whose gutters and inhabitants
alike excited my liveliest disgust. In this
street was the Eye Hospital, as was presently
testified to us by a board bearing the inscrip-
tion, *Städtische Augenklinik*.

We were taken to a dimly-lighted room in
which many people were waiting, some with
bandages over their eyes, others with all
kinds of extraordinary spectacles on, which
made them look like phantoms out of a bad
dream—nearly all more or less blind, and the
effect was surprisingly depressing.

Presently Miss Hallam and Merrick were
admitted to an inner room, and I was left
to await their return. My eye strayed over
the different faces, and I felt a sensation of
relief when I saw some one come in without

either bandage or spectacles. The new comer was a young man of middle height, and of proportions slight without being thin. There was nothing the matter with *his* eyes, unless perhaps a slight shortsightedness: he had, I thought, one of the gentlest, most attractive faces I had ever seen; boyishly open and innocent at the first glance; at the second, endued with a certain reticent calm and intellectual radiance which took away from the first youthfulness of his appearance. Soft, yet luminous brown eyes, loose brown hair hanging round his face, a certain manner which for me at least had a charm, were the characteristics of this young man. He carried a violin case, removed his hat as he came in, and being seen by one of the young men who sat at desks, took names down, and attended to people in general, was called by him:

"Herr Helfen — Herr Friedhelm Helfen!"

"*Ja—hier!*" he answered, going up to the desk, upon which there ensued a lively conversation, though carried on in a low tone, after which the young man at the desk presented a white card to "Herr Friedhelm

Helfen," and the latter, with a pleasant
" adieu," went out of the room again.

Miss Hallam and Merrick presently returned from the consulting-room, and we
went out of the dark room into the street,
which was filled with spring sunshine and
warmth : a contrast something like that between Miss Hallam's life and my own, I have
thought since. Far before us, hurrying on, I
saw the young man with the violin-case : he
turned off by the theatre, and went in at a
side door.

An hour's wandering in the *Hofgarten*—
my first view of the Rhine—a dull, flat stream
it looked, too. I have seen it since then in
mightier flow. Then we came home, and it
was decided that we should dine together
with the rest of the company at one o'clock.

A bell rang at a few minutes past one.
We went downstairs, into the room in which
I had already breakfasted, which, in general,
was known as the *Saal*. As I entered with
Miss Hallam, I was conscious that a knot of
lads or young men stood aside to let us pass,
and then giggled and scuffled behind the door
before following us into the Saal.

Two or three ladies were already seated, and an exceedingly stout lady ladled out soup at a side table, while Clara and a servant-woman carried the plates round to the different places. The stout lady turned as she saw us, and greeted us. She was Frau Steinmann, our hostess. She waited until the youths before spoken of had come in, and with a great deal of noise had seated themselves, when she began, aided by the soup-ladle, to introduce us all to each other.

We, it seemed, were to have the honour and privilege of being the only English ladies of the company. We were introduced to one or two others, and I was assigned a place by a lady introduced as Fräulein Anna Sartorius, a brunette, rather stout, with large dark eyes which looked at me in a way I did not like, a head of curly black hair cropped short, an odd brusque manner, and a something peculiar or, as she said, *selten* in her dress. This young lady sustained the introduction with self-possession and calm. It was otherwise with the young gentlemen, who appeared decidedly mixed. There were some half-dozen of them in all—a couple of English, the rest

German, Dutch, and Swedish. I had never
been in company with so many nationalities
before, and was impressed with my situation
—needlessly so.

All these young gentlemen made bows
which were, in their respective ways, triumphs
of awkwardness, with the exception of one of
our compatriots, who appeared to believe that
himself and his manners were formed to charm
and subdue the opposite sex. We then sat
down, and Fräulein Sartorius immediately
opened a conversation with me.

" *Sprechen Sie Deutsch, Fräulein?*" was her
first venture, and having received my admission that I did *not* speak a word of it, she
continued in good English :

" Now I can talk to you without offending
you. It is so dreadful when English people
who don't know German persist in thinking
that they do. There *was* an Englishwoman
here who always said *wer* when she meant
where, and *wo* when she meant who. She
said the sounds confused her."

The boys giggled at this, but the joke was
lost upon me.

" What is your name ?" she continued ;

"I didn't catch what Frau Steinmann said."

" May Wedderburn," I replied, angry with myself for blushing so excessively as I saw that all the boys held their spoons suspended, listening for my answer.

" May—*das heisst Mai*," said she, turning to the assembled youths, who testified that they were aware of it, and the Dutch boy, Brinks, inquired gutturally :

" You haf one zong in your language what calls itself ' Not always Mai,' haf you not ?"

" Yes," said I, and all the boys began to giggle as if something clever had been said. Taken all in all, what tortures have I not suffered from those dreadful boys. Shy when they ought to have been bold, and bold where a modest retiringness would better have become them. Giggling inanely at everything and nothing. Noisy and vociferous amongst themselves or with inferiors ; shy, awkward, and blushing with ladies or in refined society —distressing my feeble efforts to talk to them by their silly explosions of laughter when one of them was addressed. They formed the bane of my life for some time.

" Will you let me paint you ?" said Fräulein Sartorius, whose big eyes had been surveying me in a manner that made me nervous.

" Paint me ?"

" Your likeness, I mean. You are very pretty, and we never see that colour of hair here."

" Are you a painter ?"

" No, I'm only a *Studentin* yet ; but I paint from models. Well, will you sit to me ?"

" Oh, I don't know. If I have time, perhaps."

" What will you do to make you not have time ?"

I did not feel disposed to gratify her curiosity, and said I did not know yet what I should do.

For a short time she asked no more questions, then :

" Do you like town or country best ?"

" I don't know. I have never lived in a town."

" Do you like amusements—concerts, and theatre, and opera ?"

" I don't know," I was reluctantly obliged

to confess, for I saw that the assembled youths, though not looking at me openly, and apparently entirely engrossed with their dinners, were listening attentively to what passed.

" *You don't know,*" repeated Fräulein Sartorius, quickly seeing through my thin assumption of indifference, and proceeding to draw me out as much as possible. I wished Adelaide had been there to beat her from the field. She would have done it better than I could.

" No ; because I have never been to any."

"Haven't you ? How odd ! How very odd ! Isn't it strange ?" she added, appealing to the boys. " Fräulein has never been to a theatre or a concert."

I disdained to remark that my words were being perverted, but the game instinct rose in me. Raising my voice a little, I remarked :

" It is evident that I have not enjoyed your advantages, but I trust that the gentlemen " (with a bow to the listening boys) " will make allowances for the difference between us."

The young gentlemen burst into a chorus of delighted giggles, and Anna, shooting a rapid glance at me, made a slight grimace, but looked not at all displeased. I was, though, mightily; but, elate with victory, I turned to my compatriot at the other end of the table, and asked him at what time of the year Elberthal was pleasantest.

" Oh," said he, " it's always pleasant to me, but that's owing to myself. I make it so."

Just then, several of the other lads rose, pushing their chairs back with a great clatter, bowing to the assembled company, and saying " *Gesegnete Mahlzeit !*" as they went out.

" Why are they going, and what do they say ?" I inquired of Miss Sartorius, who replied quite amiably :

" They are students at the *Realschule.* They have to be there at two o'clock, and they say, ' Blessed be the meal-time !' as they go out."

" Do they ? How nice !" I could not help saying.

" Would you like to go for a walk this afternoon ?" said she.

" Oh, *very* much !" I had exclaimed, before I remembered that I did not like her, and did not intend to like her. " If Miss Hallam can spare me," I added.

" Oh, I think she will. I shall be ready at half-past two; then we shall return for coffee at four. I will knock at your door at the time."

On consulting Miss Hallam after dinner, I found she was quite willing for me to go out with Anna, and at the time appointed we set out.

Anna took me a tour round the town, showed me the lions, and gave me topographical details. She showed me the big, plain barrack, and the desert waste of the *Exerzierplatz* spreading before it. She did her best to entertain me, and I, with a childish prejudice against her abrupt manner, and the free, somewhat challenging look of her black eyes, was reserved, unresponsive, stupid. I took a prejudice against her—I own it—and for that and other sins committed against a woman who would have been my friend if I would have let her, I say humbly, *Mea culpa !*

" It seems a dull kind of place," said I.

" It need not be. You have advantages here which you can't get everywhere. I have been here several years, and as I have no other home I rather think I shall live here."

" Oh, indeed."

" You have a home, I suppose ?"

" Of course."

" Brothers and sisters ?"

" Two sisters," I replied, mightily ruffled by what I chose to consider her curiosity and impertinence ; though, when I looked at her, I saw what I could not but confess to be a real, and not unkind interest in her plain face and big eyes.

" Ah ! I have no brothers and sisters. I have only a little house in the country, and as I have always lived in a town, I don't care for the country. It is so lonely. The people are so stupid too—not always though. You were offended with me at dinner, *nicht wahr* ?"

" Oh dear no !" said I, very awkwardly and very untruly. The truth was, I did not like her, and was too young, too ignorant and *gauche* to try to smooth over my dislike. I did not know the pain I was giving, and if I had, should perhaps not have behaved differently.

"*Doch!*" she said, smiling. "But I did not know what a child you were, or I should have let you alone."

More offended than ever, I maintained silence. If I were certainly touchy and ill to please, Fräulein Sartorius, it must be owned, did not know how to apologise gracefully. I have since, with wider knowledge of her country and its men and women, got to see that what made her so inharmonious was, that she had a woman's form, and a man's disposition and love of freedom. As her countrywomen taken in the gross are the most utterly "in bonds" of any women in Europe, this spoiled her life in a manner which cannot be understood here, where women in comparison are free as air, and gave no little of the brusqueness and rough-ness to her manner. In an enlightened English home she would have been an admir able, firm, clever woman; here she was that most dreadful of all abnormal growths—a woman with a will of her own.

"What do they do here?" I inquired indifferently.

"Oh, many things. Though it is not a large town, there is a School of Art, which brings many painters here. There are a hundred and fifty—besides students."

"And you are a student?"

"Yes. One must have something to do—some *carrière*—though my countrywomen say not. I shall go away for a few months soon, but I am waiting for the last great concert. It will be the 'Paradise Lost' of Rubinstein." •

"Ah, yes!" said I politely, but without interest. I had never heard of Rubinstein and the *Verlorenes Paradies*. Before the furore of 1876, how many scores of provincial English *had?*

"There is very much music here," she continued. "Are you fond of it?"

"Ye-es. I can't play much, but I can sing. I have come here partly to take singing lessons."

"So!"

"Who is the best teacher?" was my next ingenuous question.

She laughed.

"That depends upon what you want to learn. There are so many; violin, *Clavier*, that is piano, flute, *'cello*, everything."

"Oh!" I replied, and asked no more questions about music; but inquired if it were pleasant at Frau Steinmann's.

She shrugged her shoulders.

"Is it pleasant anywhere? I don't find many places pleasant, because I cannot be a humbug, so others do not like me. But I believe some people like Elberthal very well. There is the theatre—that makes another element. And there are the soldiers and *Kaufleute*—merchants, I mean, so you see there is variety, though it is a small place."

"Ah, yes!" said I, looking about me as we passed down a very busy street, and I glanced to right and left with the image of Eugen Courvoisier ever distinctly if unconfessedly present to my mental view. Did he live at Elberthal? and if so, did he belong to any of those various callings? What was he? An artist who painted pictures for his bread? I thought that very probable. There was something free and artist-like in his manner, in his

loose waving hair and in his keen suscepti-
bility to beauty. I thought of his emotion
at hearing that glorious Bach music. Or was
he a musician—what Anna Sartorius called
ein Musiker? But no. My ideas of
musicians were somewhat hazy, not to say
utterly chaotic; they embraced only two
classes; those who performed or gave lessons,
and those who composed. I had never
formed to myself the faintest idea of a composer, and my experience of teachers and
performers was limited to one specimen—Mr.
Smythe of Darton, whose method and per-
formances would, as I have since learnt, have
made the hair of a musician stand horrent on
end. No—I did not think he was a musician.
An actor? Perish the thought, was my
inevitable mental answer. How should I be
able to make any better one? A soldier,
then? At that moment we met a mounted
Captain of Uhlans, harness clanking, accoutre-
ments rattling. He was apparently an acquaintance of my companion, for he saluted
with a grave politeness which sat well upon
him. Decidedly Eugen Courvoisier had the
air of a soldier. That accounted for all. No

doubt he was a soldier. In my ignorance of the strictness of German military regulations as regards the wearing of uniform, I overlooked the fact that he had been in civilian's dress, and remained delighted with my new idea: Captain Courvoisier. "What is the German for Captain?" I inquired abruptly.

"*Hauptmann.*"

"Thank you." Hauptmann Eugen Courvoisier—a noble and a gallant title, and one which became him. "How much is a thaler?" was my next question.

"It is as much as three shillings in your money."

"Oh, thank you," said I, and did a little sum in my own mind. At that rate then, I owed Herr Courvoisier the sum of ten shillings. How glad I was to find it came within my means.

As I took off my things, I wondered when Herr Courvoisier would "make out his accounts." I trusted soon.

CHAPTER III.

" Probe zum verlorenen Paradiese."

MISS HALLAM fulfilled her promise with regard to my singing lessons. She had a conversation with Fräulein Sartorius, to whom, unpopular as she was, I noticed people constantly and almost instinctively went when in need of precise information or a slight dose of common sense and clear-headedness.

Miss Hallam inquired who was the best master.

" For singing, the Herr Direktor," replied Anna very promptly. " And then he directs the best of the musical *Vereine*—the clubs—societies, whatever you name them. At least he might try Miss Wedderburn's voice."

"Who is he?"

"The head of anything belonging to music in the town—*königlicher Musik-direktor.* He conducts all the great concerts, and though he does not sing himself, yet he is one of the best teachers in the province. Lots of people come and stay here on purpose to learn from him."

"And what are these *Vereins?*"

"Every season there are six great concerts given, and a seventh for the benefit of the Direktor. The orchestra and chorus together are called a *Verein—Musik-verein.* The chorus is chiefly composed of ladies and gentlemen—amateurs, you know—*Dilettanten.* The Herr Direktor is very particular about voices. You pay so much for admission, and receive a card for the season. Then you have all the good teaching—the *Proben.*"

"What *is* a Probe?" I demanded hastily, remembering that Courvoisier had used the word.

"What you call a rehearsal."

Ah! then he was musical. At last I had found it out. Perhaps *he* was one of the amateurs who sang at these concerts, and if so, I might see him again, and if so— But Anna went on :

" It is a very good thing for any one, particularly with such a teacher as Von Francius."

" You must join," said Miss Hallam to me.

" There is Probe to-night to Rubinstein's ' Paradise Lost,' " said Anna. " I shall go, not to sing, but to listen. I can take Miss Wedderburn, if you like, and introduce her to Herr Von Francius, whom I know."

" Very nice ! very much obliged to you. Certainly," said Miss Hallam.

The Probe was fixed for seven, and shortly after that time we set off for the *Tonhalle,* or concert-hall, in which it was held.

" We shall be much too early," said she. " But the people are shamefully late. Most of them only come to *klatsch,* and flirt, or try to flirt, with the Herr Direktor."

This threw upon my mind a new light as to the Herr Direktor, and I walked by her side much impressed. She told me that if accepted I might even sing in the concert itself, as there had only been four Proben so far, and there were still several before the " Haupt-probe."

" What is the 'Haupt-probe?'" I inquired.

" General Rehearsal — when Herr Von Francius is most unmerciful to his stupid pupils. I always attend that. I like to hear him make sport of them, and then the instrumentalists laugh at them. Von Francius *never* flatters."

Inspired with nightmare-like ideas as to this terrible " Haupt-probe," I found myself, with Anna, turning into a low-fronted building inscribed *Städtische Tonhalle*, the concert-hall of the good town of Elberthal.

" This way," said she. " It is in the Rittersaal. We don't go to the large saal till the Haupt-probe."

I followed her into a long, rather shabby-looking room, at one end of which was a low orchestra, about which were dotted the desks of the absent instrumentalists, and some stiff-looking *Celli* and *Contrabassi* kept watch from a wall. On the orchestra was already assembled a goodly number of young men and women, all in lively conversation, loud laughter, and apparently high good-humour with themselves and everything in the world.

A young man with a fuzz of hair standing off about a sad and depressed-looking countenance was stealing " in and out and round about," and distributing sheets of score to the company. In the conductor's place was a tall man in grey clothes, who leaned negligently against the rail, and held a conversation with a pretty young lady, who seemed much pleased with his attention. It did not strike me at first that this was the terrible *Direktor* of whom I had been hearing. He was young, had a slender, graceful figure, and an exceedingly handsome, though (I thought at first) an unpleasing face. There was something in his attitude and manner which at first I did not quite like. Anna walked up the room, and pausing before the estrade, said :

" Herr Direktor !"

He turned : his eyes fell upon her face, and left it instantly to look at mine. Gathering himself together into a more ceremonious attitude, he descended from his estrade, and stood beside us, a little to one side, looking at us with a leisurely calmness which made me feel, I knew not why, uncomfortable. Meanwhile, Anna took up her parable.

"May I introduce the young lady? Miss Wedderburn, Herr Musik-direktor von Francius. Miss Wedderburn wishes to join the *Verein*, if you think her voice will pass. Perhaps you will allow her to sing to-night?"

"Certainly, *mein Fräulein*," said he to me, not to Anna. He had a long, rather Jewish-looking face, black hair, eyes, and moustache. The features were thin, fine, and pointed. The thing which most struck me then, at any rate, was a certain expression which, conquering all others, dominated them—at once a hardness and a hardihood which impressed me disagreeably then, though I afterwards learnt, in knowing the man, to know much more truly the real meaning of that unflinching gaze and iron look.

"Your voice is what, *mein Fräulein?*" he asked.

"Soprano."

"Sopran? We will see. The Soprani sit

over there, if you will have the goodness."

He pointed to the left of the orchestra,
and called out to the melancholy-looking
young man, " Herr Schönfeld, a chair for the
young lady !"

Herr von Francius then ascended the
orchestra himself, went to the piano, and,
after a few directions, gave us the signal to
begin. Till that day — I confess it with
shame—I had never heard of the *Verlorenes
Paradies.* It came upon me like a revelation.
I sang my best, substituting *do, re, mi,* etc.,
for the German words. Once or twice, as
Herr von Francius' forefinger beat time, I
thought I saw his head turn a little in our
direction, but I scarcely heeded it. When
the first chorus was over, he turned to me :

" You have not sung in a chorus before ?"

" No."

" So ! I should like to hear you sing
something *sola.*" He pushed towards me a
pile of music, and while the others stood
looking on and whispering amongst themselves, he went on, " Those are all sopran
songs. Select one, if you please, and try it."

Not at all aware that the incident was considered unprecedented, and was creating a sensation, I turned over the music, seeking something I knew, but could find nothing. All in German, and all strange. Suddenly I came upon one entitled, *Blute nur, liebes Herz,* the sopran solo which I had heard as I sat with Courvoisier in the cathedral. It seemed almost like an old friend. I opened it, and found it had also English words. That decided me.

"I will try this," said I, showing it to him.

He smiled. "*'S ist gut!*" Then he read the title of the song aloud, and there was a general titter, as if some very great joke were in agitation, and were much appreciated. Indeed I found that in general the jokes of the Herr Direktor, when he condescended to make any, were very keenly relished by at least the lady part of his pupils.

Not understanding the reason of the titter I took the music in my hand, and waiting for a moment until he gave me the signal, sang it after the best wise I could—not *very* brilliantly, I dare say, but with at least all my heart poured

into it. I had one requisite at least of an
artist nature—I could abstract myself upon
occasion completely from my surroundings.
I did so now. It was too beautiful, too grand.
I remembered that afternoon at Köln—the
golden sunshine streaming through the painted
windows, the flood of melody poured forth
by the invisible singer; above all, I remembered who had been by my side, and I felt as
if again beside him—again influenced by the
unusual beauty of his face and mien, and by
his clear, strange, commanding eyes. It all
came back to me—the strangest, happiest
day of my life. I sang as I had never
sung before—as I had not known I *could*
sing.

When I stopped, the tittering had ceased :
silence saluted me. The young ladies were
all looking at me : some of them had put on
their eye-glasses ; others stared at me as if I
were some strange animal from a menagerie.
The young gentlemen were whispering
amongst themselves and taking sidelong
glances at me. I scarcely heeded anything
of it. I fixed my eyes upon the judge who
had been listening to my performance—upon

Von Francius. He was pulling his moustache and at first made no remark.

" You have sung that song before, *gnädiges Fräulein ?*"

" No. I have heard it once. I have not seen the music before."

" So !" He bowed slightly, and turning once more to the others, said :

" We will begin the next chorus. Chorus of the Damned. Now, *meine Herrschaften,* I would wish to impress upon you one thing, if I can, that is—Silence, *meine Herren !*" he called sharply towards the tenors, who were giggling inanely amongst themselves. " A chorus of damned souls," he proceeded composedly, " would not sing in the same unruffled manner as a young lady who warbles, ' Spring is come—tra la la ! Spring is come— lira, lira !' in her mamma's drawing-room. Try to imagine yourself struggling in the tortures of hell——" (a delighted giggle, and a sort of " Oh, you dear, wicked man !" expression on the part of the young ladies ; a nudging of each other on that of the young gentlemen), " and *sing as if you were damned.*"

Scarcely any one seemed to take the matter

the least earnestly. The young ladies continued to giggle, and the young gentlemen to
nudge each other. Little enough of expression, if plenty of noise, was there in that
magnificent and truly difficult passage, the
changing choruses of the Condemned and
the Blessed ones—with its crowning "WEH!"
thundering down from highest sopran to
deepest bass.

" Lots of noise, and no meaning," observed
the conductor, leaning himself against the rail
of the estrade, face to his audience, folding
his arms and surveying them all one after the
other with cold self-possession. It struck me
that he despised them while he condescended
to instruct them. The power of the man
struck me again. I began to like him better.
At least I venerated his thorough understanding of what was to me a splendid
mystery. No softening appeared in the
master's eyes in answer to the rows of pretty
appealing faces turned to him ; no smile upon
his contemptuous lips responded to the eyes
—black, brown, grey, blue, yellow—all turned
with such affecting devotion to his own. Composing himself in an insouciant attitude, he

began in a cool, indifferent voice, which had, however, certain caustic tones in it which stung *me* at least to the quick :

" I never heard anything worse, even from you. My honoured Fräulein ; my *gnädigen Herren;* just try *once* to imagine what you are singing about ! It is not an exercise—it is not a love song, either of which you would no doubt perform excellently. Conceive what is happening ! Put yourself back into those mythical times. Believe, for this evening, in the story of the forfeited Paradise. There is strife between the Blessed and the Damned ; the obedient and the disobedient. There are thick clouds in the heavens—smoke, fire, and sulphur—a clashing of swords in the serried ranks of the angels : cannot you see Michael, Gabriel, Raphael, leading the heavenly host ? Cannot some of you sympathise a little with *Satan* and his struggle ?"

Looking at him, I thought they must indeed be an unimaginative set ! in that dark face before them was Mephistopheles at least —*der Geist der stets verneint*—if nothing more violent. His cool, scornful features were lit up with some of the excitement which he

could not drill into the assemblage before
him. Had he been gifted with the requisite
organ he would have acted and sung the chief
character in *Faust con amore.*

"*Ach, um Gotteswillen!*" he went on,
shrugging his shoulders, "try to forget what
you are! Try to forget that none of you
ever had a wicked thought or an unholy as-
piration——"

("Don't they see how he is laughing at
them?" I wondered.)

"You, chorus of the Condemned, try to
conjure up every wicked thought you can, and
let it come out in your voices—you who sing
the strains of the blessed ones, think of what
blessedness is. Surely each of you has his
own idea! Some of you may agree with
Lenore :

> "'Bei ihm, bei ihm ist Seligkeit,
> Und ohne Wilhelm Hölle!'

If so, think of *him;* think of *her*—only sing
it, whatever it is. Remember the strongest
of feelings :

> "'Die Engel nennen es Himmelsfreude
> Die Teufel nennen es Höllenqual,
> Die Menschen nennen es—LIEBE!'

And sing it!"

He had not become loud or excited in voice
or gesticulation, but his words, flung at them
like so many scornful little bullets, the indifferent resignation of his attitude, had their
effect upon the crew of giggling, simpering
girls and awkward, self-conscious young men.
Some idea seemed vouchsafed to them that
perhaps their performance had not been *quite*
all that it might have been ; they began in a
little more earnest, and the chorus went
better.

For my own part, I was deeply moved.
A vague excitement, a wild, and not altogether a holy one, had stolen over me. I
understood now how the man might have
influence. I bent to the power of his will,
which reached me where I stood in the background, from his dark eyes, which turned for
a moment to me now and then. It was that
will of his which put me as it were suddenly
into the spirit of the music, and revealed to
me depths in my own heart, at which I had
never even guessed. Excited, with cheeks
burning and my heart hot within me, I
followed his words and his gestures, and grew
so impatient of the dull stupidity of the

others, that tears came to my eyes. How
could that young woman, in the midst of a
sublime chorus, deliberately pause, arrange
the knot of her necktie, and then, after a
smile and a side-glance at the conductor, go
on again with a more self-satisfied simper
than ever upon her lips? What might not
the thing be with a whole chorus of sympathetic singers? The very dulness which in
fact prevailed revealed to me great regions
of possible splendour, almost too vast to think
of.

At last it was over. I turned to the
Direktor, who was still near the piano, and
asked timidly:

"Do you think I may join? Will my
voice do?"

An odd expression crossed his face; he
answered dryly:

"You may join the *Verein, mein Fräulein*—yes. Please come this way with me.
Pardon, Fräulein Stockhausen — another
time. I am sorry to say I have business at
present."

A black look from a pretty brunette, who
had advanced with an engaging smile and

an open score to ask him some question,
greeted this very composed rebuff of her
advance. The black look was directed at me
—guiltless.

Without taking any notice of the other,
he led Anna and me to a small inner room,
where there was a desk and writing materials.

"Your name, if you will be good
enough."

"Wedderburn."

"Your *Vorname*, though — your first
name."

"My christian name—oh, May."

"M—a—*na!* Perhaps you will be so
good as to write it yourself, and the street
and number of the house in which you
live."

I complied.

"Have you been here long ?"

"Not quite a week."

"Do you intend to make any stay ?"

"Some months, probably."

"Humph! If you wish to make any
progress in music, you must stay much
longer."

" It—I—it depends upon other people how long I remain."

He smiled slightly, and his smile was not unpleasant; lighted up the darkness of his face in an agreeable manner.

"So I should suppose. I will call upon you to-morrow at four in the afternoon. I should like to have a little conversation with you about your voice. Adieu, *meine Damen.*"

With a slight bow which sufficiently dismissed us, he turned to the desk again, and we went away.

Our homeward walk was a somewhat silent one. Anna certainly asked me suddenly where I had learnt to sing.

" I have not learnt properly. I can't help singing."

" I did not know you had a voice like that," said she, again.

" Like what ?"

" Herr von Francius will tell you all about it to-morrow," said she abruptly.

" What a strange man Herr von Francius is !" said I. " Is he clever ?"

" Oh, very clever."

" At first I did not like him. Now I think I do, though."

She made no answer for a few minutes; then said :

" He is an excellent teacher."

CHAPTER IV.

HERR VON FRANCIUS.

WHEN Miss Hallam heard from Anna Sartorius that my singing had evidently struck Herr von Francius, and of his intended visit, she looked pleased —so pleased that I was surprised.

He came the following afternoon, at the time he had specified. Now, in the broad daylight, and apart from his official, professional manner, I found the Herr Direktor still different from the man of last night, and yet the same. He looked even younger now than on the estrade last night, and quiet though his demeanour was, attuned to a gentlemanly calm and evenness, there was still the one thing, the cool, hard glance left,

to unite him with the dark, somewhat
sinister-looking personage who had cast his
eyes round our circle last night, and told us
to sing as if we were damned.

"Miss Hallam, this is Herr von Francius,"
said I. "He speaks English," I added.

Von Francius glanced from her to me with
a somewhat inquiring expression.

Miss Hallam received him graciously, and
they talked about all sorts of trifles, whilst I
sat by in seemly silence, till at last Miss
Hallam said :

"Can you give me any opinion upon Miss
Wedderburn's voice ?"

"Scarcely, until I have given it another
trial. She seems to have had no training."

"No, that is true," she said, and proceeded
to inform him casually that she wished me
to have every advantage I could get from
my stay in Elberthal, and must put the matter
into his hands. Von Francius looked pleased.

For my part, I was deeply moved. Miss
Hallam's generosity to one so stupid and
ignorant touched me nearly.

Von Francius, pausing a short time, at last
said :

"I must try her voice again, as I remarked. Last night I was struck with her sense of the dramatic point of what we were singing—a quality which I do not too often find in my pupils. I think, *mein Fräulein,* that with care and study, you might take a place on the stage."

"The stage!" I repeated, startled, and thinking of Courvoisier's words.

But Von Francius had been reckoning without his host. When Miss Hallam spoke of "putting the matter into his hands," she understood the words in her own sense.

"The stage!" said she, with a slight shiver. "That is quite out of the question. Miss Wedderburn is a young lady—not an actress."

"So! Then it is impossible to be both in your country?" said he, with polite sarcasm. "I spoke as simple *Künstler*—artist—I was not thinking of anything else. I do not think the *gnädiges Fräulein* will ever make a good singer of mere songs. She requires emotion to bring out her best powers—a little passion—a little scope for acting and *abandon* before she can attain the full extent of her talent."

He spoke in the most perfectly matter-of-fact way, and I trembled. I feared lest this display of what Miss Hallam would consider little short of indecent laxity and Bohemianism, would shock her so much that I should lose everything by it. It was not so, however.

"Passion—*abandon!* I think you *cannot* understand what you are talking about!" said she. "My dear sir, you must understand that those kind of things may be all very well for one set of people, but not for that class to which Miss Wedderburn belongs. Her father is a clergyman"—Von Francius bowed, as if he did not quite see what that had to do with it—"in short, *that* idea is impossible. I tell you plainly. She may learn as much as she likes, but she will never be allowed to go upon the stage."

"Then she may teach?" said he inquiringly.

"Certainly. I believe that is what she wishes to do, in case—if necessary."

"She may teach, but she may not act,"

said he reflectively. " So be it, then !
Only," he added, as if making a last effort,
" I would just mention that, apart from
artistic considerations, while a lady may wear
herself out as a poorly-paid teacher, a *prima
donna*——"

Miss Hallam smiled with calm disdain.

" It is not of the least use to speak of such
a thing. You and I look at the matter from
quite different points of view, and to argue
about it would only be to waste time."

Von Francius, with a sarcastic, ambiguous
smile, turned to me :

" And you, *mein Fräulein ?*"

" I—no. I agree with Miss Hallam," I
murmured, not really having found myself able to think about it at all, but conscious that opposition was useless. And,
besides, I did shrink away from the ideas
conjured up by that word, " the stage."

" So !" said he, with a little bow and a half
smile. " *Also!* I must try to make the
round man fit into the square hole. The first
thing will be another trial of your voice ;
then I must see how many lessons a week
you will require, and must give you instruc-

tions about practising. You must understand
that it is not pleasure or child's play which
you are undertaking. It is a work in order
to accomplish which you must strain every
nerve, and give up everything which in any
way interferes with it."

"I don't know whether I shall have time
for it," I murmured, looking doubtfully towards Miss Hallam.

"Yes, May; you will have time for it,"
was all she said.

"Is there a piano in the house?" said Von
Francius. "But, yes, certainly. Fräulein
Sartorius has one; she will lend it to us for
half an hour. If you are at liberty, *mein
Fräulein,* just now——"

"Certainly," said I, following him, as he told
Miss Hallam that he would see her again.

As he knocked at the door of Anna's
sitting-room, she came out, dressed for
walking.

"*Ach, Fräulein!* will you allow us the use
of your piano for a few minutes?"

"*Bitte!*" said she, motioning us into the
room. "I am sorry I have an engagement,
and must leave you."

" Do not let us keep you on *any* account,"
said he, with touching politeness; and she
went out.

" *Desto besser !*" he observed, shrugging his
shoulders.

He pulled off his gloves with rather an
impatient gesture, seated himself at the piano,
and struck some chords, in an annoyed
manner.

" Who is that old lady?" he inquired, looking up at me. " Any relation of yours ?"

" No—oh no ! I am her companion."

" So ! And you mean to let her prevent
you from following the career you have a
talent for ?"

" If I do not do as she wishes, I shall have
no chance of following any career at all," said
I. " And, besides, how does any one know
that I *have* a talent—for—for—what you
say ?"

" I know it ; that is why I said it. I wish
I could persuade that old lady to my way of
thinking!" he added. " I wish you were out of
her hands and in mine. *Na !* we shall see !"

It was not a very long "trial" that he gave
me ; we soon rose from the piano.

" To-morrow at eleven I come to give you a lesson," said he. " I am going to talk to Miss Hallam now. You please not come. I wish to see her alone ; and I can manage her better by myself, *nicht wahr !*"

" Thank you," said I in a subdued tone.

" You must have a piano, too," he added ; " and we must have the room to ourselves. I allow no third person to be present in my private lessons ; but go on the principle of Paul Heyse's hero, Edwin, either in open lecture, or *unter vier Augen.*"

With that he held the door open for me, and as I turned into my room, shook hands with me in a friendly manner, bidding me expect him on the morrow.

Certainly, I decided, Herr von Francius was quite unlike any one I had ever seen before ; and how *awfully* cool he was, and self-possessed. I liked him well, though.

The next morning Herr von Francius gave me my first lesson, and after that I had one from him nearly every day. As teacher and as acquaintance he was, as it were, two different men. As teacher he was strict, severe, gave much blame and little praise ; but when

he did once praise me, I remember, I carried
the remembrance of it with me for days, as a
ray of sunshine. He seemed never surprised
to find how much work had been prepared
for him, although he would express displeasure sometimes at its quality. He was a
teacher whom it was impossible not to respect, whom one obeyed by instinct. As
man, as acquaintance, I knew little of him,
though I heard much—idle tales, which it
would be as idle to repeat. They chiefly
related to his domineering disposition and
determination to go his own way, and dis-
regard that of others. In this fashion my
life became busy enough.

CHAPTER V.

" LOHENGRIN."

AS time went on, the image of Eugen Courvoisier, my unspoken of, unguessed at, friend, did *not* fade from my memory. It grew stronger. I thought of him every day—never went out without a distinct hope that I might see him; never came in without vivid disappointment that I had not seen him. I carried three thalers ten groschen so arranged in my purse that I could lay my hand upon them at a moment's notice, for as the days went on, it appeared that Herr Courvoisier had not made up his accounts, or if he had, had not chosen to claim that part of them owed by me.

I did not see him. I began dismally to
think that after all the whole thing was at an
end. He did not live at Elberthal—he had
certainly never told me that he did, I re-
minded myself. He had gone about his
business and interests — had forgotten the
waif he had helped one spring afternoon, and
I should never see him again. My heart fell,
and sank with a reasonless, aimless pang.
What did it, could it, ought it to matter to
me whether I ever saw him again or not?
Nothing, certainly, and yet I troubled myself
about it a great deal. I made little dramas
in my mind of how he and I were to meet,
and how I *would* exert my will, and make
him take the money. Whenever I saw an
unusually large or handsome house, I instantly
fell to wondering if it were his, and sometimes
made inquiries as to the owner of any particularly eligible residence. I heard of
Brauns, Müllers, Piepers, Schmidts, and the
like, as owners of the same—never the name
Courvoisier. He had disappeared—I feared
for ever.

Coming in weary one day from the town,
where I had been striving to make myself

understood in shops, I was met by Anna
Sartorius on the stairs. She had not yet
ceased to be civil to me—civil, that is, in her
way—and my unreasoning aversion to her
was as great as ever.

" This is the last opera of the season," said
she, displaying a pink ticket. " I am glad
you will get to see one, as the theatre closes
after to-night."

" But I am not going."

" Yes, you are. Miss Hallam has a ticket
for you. I am going to chaperon you."

" I must go and see about that," said I
hastily, rushing upstairs.

The news, incredible though it seemed, was
quite true. The ticket lay there. I picked
it up and gazed at it fondly. *Stadttheater
zu Elberthal. Parquet, No.* 16. As I had
never been in a theatre in my life, this con-
veyed no distinct idea to my mind, but it was
quite enough for me that I was going. The
rest of the party, I found, were to consist of
Vincent, the Englishman, Anna Sartorius,
and the Dutch boy, Brinks.

It was Friday evening, and the opera was
Lohengrin. I knew nothing, then, about

different operatic styles, and my ideas of operatic music were based upon duets upon selected airs from *La Traviata, La Sonnambula,* and *Lucia.* I thought the story of *Lohengrin,* as related by Vincent, interesting. I was not in the least aware that my first opera was to be a different one from that of most English girls. Since, I have wondered sometimes what would be the result upon the musical taste of a person who was put through a course of Wagnerian opera *first,* and then turned over to the Italian school—leaving Mozart, Beethoven, Glück to take care of themselves, as they may very well do— thus exactly reversing the usual (English) process.

Anna was very quiet that evening. Afterwards I knew that she must have been observing me. We were in the first row of the *Parquet,* with the orchestra alone between us and the stage. I was fully occupied in looking about me—now at the curtain hiding the great mystery, now behind and above me at the boxes, in a youthful state of ever-increasing hope and expectation.

" We are very early," said Vincent, who

was next to me, "very early, and very near,"
he added, but he did not seem much distressed
at either circumstance.

Then the gas was suddenly turned up quite
high. The bustle increased cheerfully. The
old, young, and middle-aged ladies who filled
the *Logen* in the *Erster Rang*—hardened
theatre-goers, who came as regularly every
night in the week during the eight months of
the season as they ate their breakfasts and
went to their beds, were gossiping with the
utmost violence, exchanging nods and odd
little old-fashioned bows with other ladies in
all parts of the house, leaning over to look
whether the *Parquet* was well filled, and
remarking that there were more people in the
Balcon than usual. The musicians were
dropping into the orchestra. I was startled
to see a face I knew—that pleasant-looking
young violinist with the brown eyes, whose
name I had heard called out at the Eye
Hospital. They all seemed very fond of him,
particularly a man who struggled about with
a violoncello, and who seemed to have a series
of jokes to relate to Herr Helfen, exploding
with laughter, and every now and then shaking

the loose thick hair from his handsome, genial
face. Helfen listened to him with a half-
smile, screwing up his violin and giving him
a quiet look now and then. The inspiring
noise of tuning-up had begun, and I was on
the very tiptoe of expectation.

As I turned once more and looked round,
Vincent said, laughing, "Miss Wedderburn,
your hat has hit me three times in the face."
It was, by-the-bye, *the* brown hat which had
graced my head that day at Köln.

"Oh, has it? I beg your pardon!" said I,
laughing too, as I brought my eyes again
to bear upon the stage. "The seats are too
near toge—"

Further words were upon my lips, but they
were never uttered. In roving across the
orchestra to the foot-lights, my eyes were
arrested. In the well of the orchestra,
immediately before my eyes, was one empty
chair, that by right belonging to the leader
of the first violins. Freidhelm Helfen sat in
the one next below it. All the rest of the
musicians were assembled. The conductor
was in his place, and looked a little impatiently towards that empty chair. Through

a door to the left of the orchestra there came
a man, carrying a violin, and made his way,
with a nod here, a half smile there, a tap on
the shoulder in another direction. Arrived
at the empty chair, he laid his hand upon
Helfen's shoulder, and bending over him,
spoke to him as he seated himself. He kept
his hand on that shoulder, as if he liked it to
be there. Helfen's eyes said as plainly as
possible that *he* liked it. Fast friends, on the
face of it, were these two men. In this moment, though I sat still, motionless, and quiet,
I certainly realised as nearly as possible that
*im*possible sensation, the turning upside down
of the world. I did not breathe. I waited,
spell-bound, in the vague idea that my eyes
might open, and I find that I had been
dreaming. After an earnest speech to Helfen
the new-comer raised his head, and as he
shouldered his violin, his eyes travelled care-
lessly along the first row of the Parquet—*our*
row. I did not awake ; things did not melt
away in mist before my eyes. He *was* Eugen
Courvoisier, and he looked braver, hand-
somer, gallanter, and more apart from the
crowd of men now, in this moment, than even

my sentimental dreams had pictured him. I
felt it all : I also know now that it was partly
the very strength of the feeling I had—the
very intensity of the admiration which took
from me reflection and reason for the moment.
I felt as if every one must see how I felt. I
remembered that no one knew what had happened ; I dreaded lest they should. I did
the most cowardly and treacherous thing that
circumstances permitted to me—displayed to
what an extent my power of folly and stupidity
could carry me. I saw these strange, bright
eyes, whose power I felt, coming towards me.
In one second they would be upon me. I
felt myself white with anxiety. His eyes were
coming—coming—slowly, surely. They had
fallen upon Vincent, and he nodded to him.
They fell upon me. It was for the tenth of a
second only. I saw a look of recognition
flash into his eyes—upon his face. I saw he
was *going* to bow to me. With (as it seemed
to me) all the blood in my veins rushing to
my face, my head swimming, my heart beating, I dropped my eyes to the play-bill upon
my lap, and stared at the crabbed German
characters—the names of the players, the

characters they took. "Elsa—Lohengrin."
I read them again and again, while my ears
were singing, my heart beating so, and I
thought every one in the theatre knew and
was looking at me.

"Mind you listen to the overture, Miss
Wedderburn," said Vincent hastily, in my
ear, as the first liquid, yearning, long-drawn
notes sounded from the violins.

"Yes," said I, raising my face at last, and
looking, or rather feeling a look compelled
from me, to the place where he sat. This
time our eyes met fully. I do not know
what I felt when I saw him look at me as
unrecognisingly as if I had been a wooden
doll in a shop window. Was he looking past
me? No. His eyes met mine direct —
glance for glance : not a sign, not a quiver of
the mouth, not a waver of the eyelids. I
heard no more of the overture. When he
was playing, and so occupied with his music,
I observed him surreptitiously ; when he was
not playing, I kept my eyes fixed firmly upon
my play-bill. I did not know whether to
be most distressed at my own disloyalty to a
kind friend, or most appalled to find that the

man with whom I had spent a whole afternoon in the firm conviction that he was outwardly, as well as inwardly, my equal and a
gentleman—(how the tears, half of shame,
half of joy, rise to my eyes now as I think of
my poor, pedantic little scruples *then!*)—the
man of whom I had assuredly thought and
dreamed many and many a time and oft was
—a professional musician, a man in a band,
a German band, playing in the public orchestra
of a provincial town. Well! well!

In our village at home, where the popula-
tion consisted of clergymen's widows, daughters of deceased naval officers, and old women
in general, and those old women ladies of the
genteelest description—the Army and the
Church (for which I had been brought up to
have the deepest veneration and esteem, as
the two head powers in our land—for we did
not take Manchester, Birmingham, and
Liverpool into account at Skernford)—the
Army and the Church, I say, looked down a
little upon Medicine and the Law, as being
perhaps more necessary, but less select factors
in that great sum—the Nation. Medicine
and the Law looked down very decidedly

upon commercial wealth, and Commerce in her turn turned up her nose at retail establishments, while one and all—Church and Army, Law and Medicine, Commerce in the gross and Commerce in the little—united in pointing the finger at artists, musicians, literati, *et id omne genus,* considering them, with some few well-known and orthodox exceptions, as Bohemians, and calling them " persons "—a name whose mighty influence is unknown to those who never were and never will be " persons." They were a class with whom we had and could have nothing in common ; so utterly outside our life, that we scarcely ever gave a thought to their existence. We read of pictures, and wished to see them ; heard of musical wonders, and desired to hear them—*as* pictures, *as* compositions. I do not think it ever entered our heads to remember that a man with a quick life throbbing in his veins, with feelings, hopes, and fears and thoughts, painted the picture, and that in seeing it we also saw him —that a consciousness, if possible, yet more keen and vivid produced the combinations of sound which brought tears to our eyes when

we heard " the band "—beautiful abstraction !
—play them.   Certainly we never considered
the performers as anything more than people
who could play—one who blew his breath
into a brass tube, another into a wooden
pipe ; one who scraped a small fiddle with
fine strings, another who scraped a big one
with coarse strings.

I was seventeen, and not having an original
mind, had up to now judged things from
earlier teaching and impressions.   I do not
ask to be excused.   I only say that I was
ignorant, as ignorant as ever *even* a girl of
seventeen was.   I did not know the amount
of art and culture which lay amongst those
rather shabby-looking members of the Elberthal *städtische Kapelle*—did not know that
that little cherubic-faced man, who drew his
bow so lovingly across his violin, had played
under Mendelssohn's conductorship, and could
tell tales about how the master had drilled
his band, and what he had said about the
first performance of the *Lobgesang.*   The
young man to whom I had seen Courvoisier
speaking was—I learnt it later—a performer
to ravish the senses, a conductor in the true

sense—not a mere man who waves a stick up and down, but one who can put some of the meaning of the music into his gestures, and dominate his players. I did not know that the musicians before me were nearly all true artists, and some of them undoubted gentlemen to boot, even if their income averaged something under that of a skilled Lancashire operative. But even if I had known it as well as possible, and had been aware that there could be nothing derogatory in my knowing or being known by one of them, I could not have been more wretched than I was in having been, as it were, false to a friend. The dreadful thing was, or ought to be—I could not quite decide which— that such a person should have been my friend.

"How he *must* despise me!" I thought, my cheeks burning, my eyes fastened upon the play-bill. "I owe him ten shillings. If he likes he can point me out to them all and say, 'That is an English girl—lady I cannot call her. I found her quite alone and lost at Köln, and I did all I could to help her. I saved her a great deal of anxiety and inconvenience. She was not above accepting my assistance ; she confided her story very freely to me ; she is nothing very particular—has nothing to boast of—no money, no knowledge, nothing superior ; in fact, she is simple and ignorant to a quite surprising extent ; but she has just cut me dead. What do you think of her ?' "

Until the curtain went up I sat in torture. When the play began, however, even my discomfort vanished in my wonder at the spectacle. It was the first I had seen. Try to picture it, O worn-out and blasé frequenter of play and opera ! Try to realise the feelings of an impressionable young person of seventeen when *Lohengrin* was revealed to her for the first time—Lohengrin, the mystic knight, with the glamour of eld upon him—Lohengrin, sailing in blue and silver, like a dream, in his swan-drawn boat, stepping majestic forth, and speaking in a voice of purest melody, as he thanks the bird and dismisses it :

> " Dahin, woher mich trug dein Kahn
> Kehr wieder nur zu unserm Glück !
> Drum sei getreu dein Dienst gethan,
> Leb wohl, leb wohl, mein lieber Schwan."

Elsa, with the wonder, the gratitude, the love, and alas! the weakness in her eyes! The astonished Brabantine men and women. They could not have been more astonished than I was. It was all perfectly real to me. What did I know about the stage? To me, yonder figure in blue mantle and glittering armour was Lohengrin, the son of Percivale, not Herr Siegel, the first tenor of the company, who acted stiffly, and did not know what to do with his legs. The lady in black velvet and spangles, who gesticulated in a corner, was an *Edelfrau* to me, as the programme called her, not the chorus leader, with two front teeth missing, an inartistically made-up countenance, and large feet. I sat through the first act with my eyes riveted upon the stage. What a thrill shot through me as the tenor embraced the soprana, and warbled melodiously, "*Elsa, ich liebe Dich!*" My mouth and eyes were wide open, I have no doubt, till at last the curtain fell. With a long sigh I slowly brought my eyes down, and *Lohengrin* vanished like a dream. There was Eugen Courvoisier standing up—he had resumed the old attitude—was twirling his

moustache and surveying the company. Some
of the other performers were leaving the orchestra by two little doors. If only he would
go too! As I nervously contemplated a
gracefully indifferent remark to Herr Brinks,
who sat next to me, I saw Courvoisier step
forward. Was he, could he be going to speak
to me? I should have deserved it, I knew,
but I felt as if I should die under the ordeal.
I sat preternaturally still, and watched, as if
mesmerised, the approach of the musician.
He spoke again to the young man whom I
had seen before, and they both laughed.
Perhaps he had confided the whole story to
him, and was telling him to observe what he
was going to do. Then Herr Courvoisier
tapped the young man on the shoulder and
laughed again, and then he came on. He
was not looking at me; he came up to the
boarding, leaned his elbow upon it, and said
to Eustace Vincent :

"Good-evening : *wie geht's Ihnen?*"

Vincent held out his hand. "Very well,
thanks. And you? I haven't seen you
lately."

"Then you haven't been at the theatre

lately," he laughed. He never testified to me by word or look that he had even seen me before. At last I got to understand, as his eyes repeatedly fell upon me without the slightest sign of recognition, that he did not intend to claim my acquaintance. I do not know whether I was most wretched or most relieved at the discovery. It spared me a great deal of embarrassment; it filled me, too, with inward shame beyond all description. And then, too, I was dismayed to find how totally I had mistaken the position of the musician. Vincent was talking eagerly to him. They had moved a little nearer the other end of the orchestra. The young man, Helfen, had come up: others had joined them. I, meanwhile, sat still—heard every tone of his voice, took in every gesture of his head or his hand, and felt as I trust never to feel again—and yet I lived in some such feeling as that for what at least seemed to me a long time. What was the feeling that clutched me—held me fast—seemed to burn me? And what was that I heard? Vincent speaking:

" Last Thursday week, Courvoisier—why

didn't you come ? We were waiting for you."

" I missed the train."

Until now he had been speaking German, but he said this distinctly in English, and I heard every word.

" Missed the train ?" cried Vincent in his cracked voice. " Nonsense, man ! Helfen, here, and Alekotte were in time, and they had been at the Probe as much as you."

" I was detained in Köln and couldn't get back till evening," said he. " Come along, Friedel ; there's the call-bell."

I raised my eyes—met his. I do not know what expresssion was in mine. His never wavered, though he looked at me long and steadily—no glance of recognition—no sign still. I would have risked the astonishment of every one of them now, for a sign that he remembered me. None was given.

Lohengrin had no more attraction for me. I felt in pain that was almost physical, and weak with excitement as at last the curtain fell and we left our places.

" You were very quiet," said Vincent, as we walked home. " Did you not enjoy it ?"

" Very much, thank you. It was very beautiful," said I faintly.

" So Herr Courvoisier was not at the Soirée," said the loud, rough voice of Anna Sartorius.

" No," was all Vincent said.

" Did you have anything new ? Was Herr von Francius there too ?"

" Yes ; he was there too."

I pondered. Brinks whistled loudly the air of Elsa's *Brautzug,* and we paced across the Lindenallée. We had not many paces to go. The lamps were lighted, the people were thronging thick as in the day-time. The air was full of laughter, talk, whistling and humming of the airs from the opera. My ear strained eagerly through the confusion. I could have caught the faintest sound of Courvoisier's voice had it been there, but it was not. And we came home ; Vincent opened the door with his latch-key, said, " It has not been very brilliant, has it ? That tenor is a stick," and we all went to our different rooms. It was in such wise that I met Eugen Courvoisier for the second time.

CHAPTER VI.

" Will you sing ?"

THE theatre season closed with that evening on which *Lohengrin* was performed. I ran no risk of meeting Courvoisier face to face again in that alarming, sudden manner. But the subject had assumed diseased proportions in my mind. I found myself confronted with him yet, and week after week. My business in Elberthal was music—to learn as much music and hear as much music as I could : wherever there was music there was also Eugen Courvoisier —naturally. There was only one *städtische Kapelle* in Elberthal. Once a week at least —each Saturday—I saw him, and he saw me at the unfailing Instrumental Concert to

which every one in the house went, and to
absent myself from which would instantly
have set every one wondering what could be
my motive for it.   My usual companions were
Clara Steinmann, Vincent, the Englishman,
and often Frau Steinmann herself.   Anna
Sartorius and some other girl-students of art
usually brought sketch-books, and were far
too much occupied in making studies or caricatures of the audience to pay much attention
to the music.   The audience were, however,
hardened ; they were used to it.   Anna and
her friends were not alone in the practice.
There were a dozen or more artists or *soi-
disant* artists busily engaged with their
sketch-books.   The concert-room offered a
rich field to them.   One could at least be
sure of one thing—that they were *not* taking
off the persons at whom they looked most
intently.   There must be quite a gallery
hidden away in some old sketch-books—of
portraits or wicked caricatures of the audience
that frequented the concerts of the *Instrumental Musik Verein.*   I wonder where they
all are ? Who has them ? What has become of the light-hearted sketchers ? I often

recall those homely Saturday evening concerts; the long, shabby saal with its faded
out-of-date decorations; its rows of small
tables with the well-known groups around
them; the mixed and motley audience. How
easy, after a little while, to pick out the English, by their look of complacent pleasure at
the delightful ease and unceremoniousness of
the whole affair; their gladness at finding a
public entertainment where one's clothes were
not obliged to be selected with a view to out-
shining those of every one else in the room;
the students shrouded in a mystery, sacred
and impenetrable, of tobacco smoke. The
spruce-looking schoolboys from the *Gymna-
sium* and *Realschule,* the old captains and
generals, the Fräulein their daughters, the
gnädigen Frauen their wives; dressed in the
disastrous plaids, checks, and stripes, which
somehow none but German women ever get
hold of. Shades of *Le Follet!* What costumes there were on young and old for an
observing eye! What bonnets, what boots,
what stupendously daring accumulation of
colours and styles and periods of dress
crammed and piled on the person of one sub-

stantial Frau Generalin, or Doctorin or Professorin !

The low orchestra—the tall, slight, yet commanding figure of Von Francius on the estrade; his dark face with its indescribable mixture of pride, impenetrability and insouciance; the musicians behind him—every face of them as well known to the audience as those of the audience to them : it was not a mere " concert," which in England is another word for so much expense and so much vanity—it was a gathering of friends. We knew the music in which the *Kapelle* was most at home; we knew their strong points and their weak ones; the passage in the Pastoral Symphony where the second violins were a little weak ; that overture where the *Blaseinstrumente* came out so well—the symphonies one heard—the divine wealth of undying art and beauty ! Those days are past: despite what I suffered in them they had their joys for me. Yes ; I suffered at those concerts. I must ever see the one face which for me blotted out all others in the room, and endure the silent contempt which I believed I saw upon it. Probably it was my own feeling of inward self-contempt which made me believe I saw that expression there. His face had for me a miserable, basilisk-like attraction. When I was there and he was there, I must look at him and endure the silent, smiling disdain which I at least believed he bestowed upon me. How did he contrive to do it? How often our eyes met, and every time it happened he looked me full in the face, and never would give me the faintest gleam of recognition. It was as though I looked at two diamonds, which returned my stare unwinkingly and unseeingly. I managed to make myself thoroughly miserable—pale and thin with anxiety and self-reproach. I let this man, and the speculations concerning him, take up my whole thoughts, and I kept silence, because I dreaded so intensely lest any question should bring out the truth. I smiled drearily when I thought that there certainly was no danger of any one but Miss Hallam ever knowing it, for the only person who could have betrayed me chose now, of deliberate purpose, to cut me as completely as I had once cut him.

As if to show very decidedly that he *did*

intend to cut me, I met him one day, not in the street, but in the house, on the stairs. He sprang up the steps, two at a time, came to a momentary pause on the landing, and looked at me. No look of surprise, none of recognition. He raised his hat, that was nothing; in ordinary politeness he would have done it had he never seen me in his life before. The same cold, bright, *hard* glance fell upon me, keen as an eagle's, and as devoid of every gentle influence as the same.

I silently held out my hand.

He looked at it for a moment, then with a grave coolness which chilled me to the soul, murmured something about "not having the honour," bowed slightly, and stepping forward, walked into Vincent's room.

I was going to the room in which my piano stood, where I had my music lessons, for they had told me that Herr von Francius was waiting. I looked at him as I went into the room. How different he was from that other man : darker, more secret, more scornful-looking, with not less power, but so much less benevolence.

I was *distraite*, and sang exceedingly ill.

We had been going through the solo sopran
parts of the *Paradise Lost.* I believe I sang
vilely that morning. I was not thinking of
Eva's sin and the serpent, but of other things,
which, despite the story related in the Book
of Genesis, touched me more nearly. Several
times already had he made me sing through
Eva's stammering answer to her God's question :

> " Ah, Lord ! . . . The Serpent !
> The beautiful, glittering Serpent,
> With his beautiful, glittering words,
> He, Lord, did lead astray
> The weak Woman !"

" *Bah !*" exclaimed Von Francius, when I
had sung it some three or four times, each
time worse, each time more distractedly.
He flung the music upon the floor, and his
eyes flashed, startling me from my uneasy
thoughts back to the present. He was looking at me with a dark cloud upon his face.
I stared, stooped meekly, and picked up the
music.

" Fräulein, what are you dreaming about ?"
he asked impatiently. " You are not singing
Eva's shame and dawning terror as she feels

herself undone. You are singing—and badly, too—a mere sentimental song, such as any schoolgirl might stumble through. I am ashamed of you."

" I—I," stammered I, crimsoning, and ashamed for myself too.

"You were thinking of something else," he said, his brow clearing a little. " *Na!* it comes so sometimes. Something has happened to distract your attention. The amiable Miss Hallam has been a little *more* amiable than usual."

" No."

" Well, well. *'S ist mir egal.* But now, as you have wasted half an hour in vanity and vexation, will you be good enough to let your thoughts return here to me and to your duty ? or else—I must go, and leave the lesson till you are in the right voice again."

" I am all right—try me," said I, my pride rising in arms as I thought of Courvoisier's behaviour a short time ago.

" Very well. Now. You are Eva, please remember, the first woman, and you have gone wrong. Think of who is questioning you, and——"

"Oh yes, yes, I know. Please begin."

He began the accompaniment, and I sang for the fifth time Eva's scattered notes of shame and excuse.

"Brava!" said he when I had finished, and I was the more startled as he had never before given me the faintest sign of approval, but had found such constant fault with me, that I usually had a fit of weeping after my lesson; weeping with rage and disappointment at my own shortcomings.

"At last you know what it means," said he. "I always told you your forte was dramatic singing."

"Dramatic! But this is an oratorio."

"It may be called an oratorio, but it is a drama all the same. What more dramatic, for instance, than what you have just sung, and all that goes before? Now suppose we go on. I will take Adam."

Having given myself up to the music I sang my best with earnestness. When we had finished Von Francius closed the book, looked at me, and said:

"Will you sing the *Eva* music at the concert?"

"*I?*"

He bowed silently, and still kept his eyes fixed upon my face, as if to say, "Refuse if you dare!"

"I—I'm afraid I should make such a mess of it," I murmured at last.

"Why any more than to-day?"

"Oh! but all the people!" said I, expostulating; "it is so different."

He gave a little laugh of some amusement.

"How odd! and yet how like you!" said he. "Do you suppose that the people who will be at the concert will be half as much alive to your defects as I am? If you can sing before me, surely you can sing before so many rows of——"

"Cabbages? I wish I could think they were."

"Nonsense! What would be the use, where the pleasure, in singing to cabbages? I mean simply inhabitants of Elberthal. What can there be so formidable about *them?*"

I murmured something.

"Well, will you do it?"

"I am sure I should break down," said I,

trying to find some sign of relenting in his eyes. I discovered none. He was not waiting to hear whether I said " yes" or "no ;" he was waiting *until* I said " yes."

" If you did," he replied with a friendly smile, " I should never teach you another note."

" Why not ?"

" Because you would be a coward, and not worth teaching."

" But Miss Hallam ?"

" Leave her to me."

I still hesitated.

" It is the *premier pas qui coûte*," said he, still keeping a friendly but determined gaze upon my undecided face.

" I want to accustom you to appearing in public," he added. " By degrees, you know. There is nothing unusual in *Germany* for one in your position to sing in such a concert."

" I was not thinking of that ; but that it is impossible that I can sing well enough——"

" You sing well enough for my purpose. You will be amazed to find what an impetus to your studies, and what a fillip to your industry will be given by once singing before a number of other people. And then, on the stage——"

" But I am not going on the stage."

" I think you are. At least, if you do otherwise you will do wrong. You have gifts which are in themselves a responsibility."

" I—gifts—what gifts ?" I asked incredulously. " I am as stupid as a donkey. My sisters always said so, and sisters are sure to know ; you may trust them for that."

" Then you will take the sopran solos ?"

" Do you think I can ?"

" I don't *think* you can ; I say you *must.* I will call upon Miss Hallam this afternoon. And the *gage*—fee—what you call it ?—is fifty thalers."

" *What !*" I cried, my whole attitude changing to one of greedy expectation. " Shall I be *paid ?*"

" Why, *natürlich*," said he, turning over sheets of music, and averting his face to hide a smile.

" Oh ! then I will sing."

" Good ! Only please to remember that it

is my concert, and I am responsible for the
soloists ; and pray think rather more about
the beautiful glittering serpent than about
the beautiful glittering thalers."

"I can think about both," was my unholy,
time-serving reply.

Fifty thalers! Untold gold!

CHAPTER VII.

"Prinz Eugen, der edle Ritter."

T was the evening of the Haupt-probe, a fine moonlight night in the middle of May—a month since I had come to Elberthal, and it seemed so much, so very much more.

To my astonishment—and far from agree-able astonishment—Anna Sartorius informed me of her intention to accompany me to the Probe. I put objections in her way as well as I knew how, and said I did not think outsiders were admitted. She laughed, and said :

"That is too funny, that you should in-struct me in such thing. Why, I have a ticket for all the Proben, as any one can have

who chooses to pay two thalers at the *casse.*
I have a mind to hear this. They say the
orchestra are going to rebel against Von
Francius. And I am going to the concert
to-morrow, too. One cannot hear too much
of such fine music; and when one's friend
sings, too——"

"What friend of yours is going to sing ?" I
inquired coldly.

"Why, you, you *allerliebster kleiner Engel,*"
said she, in a tone of familiarity, to which I
strongly objected.

I could say no more against her going, but
certainly displayed no enthusiastic desire for
her company.

The Probe, we found, was to be in the
great Saal; it was half-lighted, and there
were perhaps some fifty people, holders of
Probe-tickets, seated in the parquet.

"You are going to sing well to-night," said
Von Francius, as he handed me up the steps
—"for my sake and your own, *nicht wahr ?*"

" I will try," said I, looking round the
great orchestra, and seeing how full it was—
so many fresh faces, both in chorus and
orchestra.

And as I looked, I saw Courvoisier come in by the little door at the top of the orchestra steps, and descend to his place. His face was clouded—very clouded; I had never seen him look thus before. He had no smile for those who greeted him. As he took his place beside Helfen, and the latter asked him some question, he stared absently at him, then answered with a look of absence and weariness.

"Herr Courvoisier," said Von Francius—and I, being near, heard the whole dialogue "you always allow yourself to be waited for."

Courvoisier glanced up. I, with a new, sudden interest, watched the behaviour of the two men. In the face of Von Francius I thought to discover dislike, contempt.

"I beg your pardon; I was detained," answered Courvoisier composedly.

"It is unfortunate that you should be so often detained at the time when your work should be beginning."

Unmoved and unchanging, Courvoisier heard and submitted to the words, and to the tone in which they were spoken—sarcastic, sneering, and unbelieving.

"Now we will begin," pursued Von Francius, with a disagreeable smile, as he rapped with his bâton upon the rail. I looked at Courvoisier—looked at his friend, Friedhelm Helfen. The former was sitting as quietly as possible, rather pale, and with the same clouded look, but not deeper than before; the latter was flushed, and eyed Von Francius with no friendly glance.

There seemed a kind of slumbering storm in the air. There was none of the lively discussion usual at the Proben. Courvoisier, first of the first violins, and from whom all the others seemed to take their tone, sat silent, grave, and still. Von Francius, though quiet, was biting. I felt afraid of him. Something must have happened to put him into that evil mood.

My part did not come until late in the second part of the oratorio. I had almost forgotten that I was to sing at all, and was watching Von Francius, and listening to his sharp speeches. I remembered what Anna Sartorius had said in describing this Hauptprobe to me. It was all just as she had said. He was severe; his speeches roused the phlegmatic blood, set the professional instrumentalists laughing at their amateur co-operators, but provoked no reply or resentment. It was extraordinary, the effect of this man's will upon those he had to do with —upon women in particular.

There was one haughty-looking blonde—a Swede—tall, majestic, with long yellow curls, and a face full of pride and high temper, who gave herself decided airs, and trusted to her beauty and insolence to carry off certain radical defects of harshness of voice and want of ear. I never forgot how she stared me down from head to foot on the occasion of my first appearance alone, as if to say, "What do *you* want here ?"

It was in vain that she looked haughty and handsome. Addressing her as Fräulein Hülström, Von Francius gave her a sharp lecture, imitated the effect of her voice in a particularly soft passage with ludicrous accuracy. The rest of the chorus was tittering audibly, the musicians, with the exception of Courvoisier and his friend, nudging each other and smiling. She bridled haughtily, flashed a furious glance at her mentor, grew crimson, received a sarcastic smile which baffled her, and subsided again.

So it was with them all. His blame was plentiful; his praise so rare as to be almost an unknown quantity. His chorus and orchestra were famed for the minute perfection and precision of their play and singing. Perhaps the performance lacked something else—passion, colour. Von Francius, at that time at least, was no genius, though his talent, his power, and his method were undeniably great. He was, however, not popular — not the Harold, the "beloved leader" of his people.

It was to-night that I was first shown how all was not smooth for him; that in this art union there were splits—"little rifts within the lute," which, should they extend, might literally in the end "make the music mute." I heard whispers around me. "Herr von Francius is angry." "*Nicht wahr?*" "Herr Courvoisier looks angry too." "Yes, he does." "There will be an open quarrel there soon." "I think so." "They are both clever; one should be less clever than the other." "They are so opposed." "Yes.

They say Courvoisier has a party of his own, and that all the orchestra are on his side." " *So !*" in accents of curiosity and astonishment. " *Ja wohl !* And that if Von Francius does not mind, he will see Herr Courvoisier in his place," etc., etc., without end. All which excited me much, as the first glimpse into the affairs of those about whom we think much and know little (a form of life well known to women in general) always does interest us.

These things made me forget to be nervous or anxious. I saw myself now as part of the whole, a unit in the sum of a life which interested me. Von Francius gave me a sign of approval when I had finished, but it was a mechanical one. He was thinking of other things.

The Probe was over. I walked slowly down the room looking for Anna Sartorius, more out of politeness than because I wished for her company. I was relieved to find that she had already gone, probably not finding all the entertainment she expected, and I was able, with a good conscience, to take my way home alone.

My way home! not yet. I was to live through something before I could take my way home.

I went out of the large saal through the long verandah into the street. A flood of moonlight silvered it. There was a laughing, chattering crowd about me—all the chorus; men and girls, going to their homes or their lodgings, in ones or twos, or in large cheerful groups. Almost opposite the *Tonhalle* was a tall house, one of a row, and of this house the lowest floor was used as a shop for antiquities, curiosities, and a thousand odds and ends useful or beautiful to artists; costumes, suits of armour, old china, anything and everything. The window was yet lighted. As I paused for a moment before taking my homeward way, I saw two men cross the moonlit street and go in at the open door of the shop. One was Courvoisier; in the other I thought to recognise Friedhelm Helfen, but was not quite sure about it. They did not go into the shop, as I saw by the bright large lamp that burned within, but along the passage and up the stairs. I followed them, resolutely beating down shyness, unwillingness, timidity. My reluctant steps took me to the window of the antiquity shop, and I stood looking in before I could make up my mind to enter. Bits of rococo ware stood in the window, majolica jugs, chased metal dishes and bowls, bits of renaissance-work, tapestry, carpet, a helm with the vizor up, gaping at me as if tired of being there. I slowly drew my purse from my pocket, put together three thalers and a ten groschen-piece, and with lingering, unwilling steps, entered the shop. A pretty young woman in a quaint dress, which somehow harmonised with the place, came forward. She looked at me as if wondering what I could possibly want. My very agitation gave calmness to my voice as I inquired :

"Does Herr Courvoisier, a *Musiker*, live here ?"

"*Ja wohl !*" answered the young woman, with a look of still greater surprise. "On the third *étage*, straight upstairs. The name is on the door."

I turned away, and went slowly up the steep wooden uncarpeted staircase. On the first landing a door opened at the sound of my footsteps, and a head was popped out—a rough, fuzzy head, with a pale, eager-looking face under the bush of hair.

"Ugh!" said the owner of this amiable visage, and shut the door with a bang. I looked at the plate upon it; it bore the legend, *Hermann Duntze, Maler.* To the second *étage.* Another door—another plate: *Bernhardt Knoop, Maler.* The house seemed to be a resort of artists. There was a lamp burning on each landing; and now, at last, with breath and heart alike failing, I ascended the last flight of stairs, and found myself upon the highest *étage* before another door, on which was roughly painted up *Eugen Courvoisier.* I looked at it with my heart beating suffocatingly. Some one had scribbled in red chalk beneath the christian name, *Prinz Eugen, der edle Ritter.* Had it been done in jest or earnest? I wondered, and then knocked. Such a knock!

"*Herein!*"

I opened the door, and stepped into a large, long, low room. On the table, in the centre, burnt a lamp, and sitting there, with the light falling upon his earnest young face, was

Helfen, the violinist, and near to him sat
Courvoisier, with a child upon his knee, a
little lad with immense dark eyes, tumbled
black hair, and flushed, just awakened face.
He was clad in his night-dress and a little
red dressing-gown, and looked like a spot of
almost feverish, quite tropic brightness, in
contrast with the grave, pale face which bent
over him.   Courvoisier held the two delicate
little hands in one of his own, and was looking down with love unutterable upon the
beautiful, dazzling child-face.   Despite the
different complexion and a different style of
feature too, there was so great a likeness in
the two faces, particularly in the broad, noble
brow, as to leave no doubt of the relation-
ship.   My musician and the boy were father
and son.

Courvoisier looked up as I came in.   For
one half moment there leapt into his eyes a
look of surprise and of something more.   If
it had lasted a second longer I could have
sworn it was welcome—then it was gone.
He rose, turned the child over to Helfen,
saying, " One moment, Friedel," then turned
to me as to some stranger who had come on

an errand as yet unknown to him, and did not speak. The little one, from Helfen's knee, stared at me with large, solemn eyes, and Helfen himself looked scarcely less impressed.

I have no doubt I looked frightened—I felt so—frightened out of my senses. I came tremulously forward, and offering my pieces of silver, said in the smallest voice which I had ever used :

" I have come to pay my debt. I did not know where you lived, or I should have done it long before."

He made no motion to take the money, but said—I almost started, so altered was the voice from that of my frank companion at Köln, to an icy coldness of ceremony :

" *Mein Fräulein,* I do not understand."

" You—you—the things you paid for. Do you not remember me ?"

" Remember a lady who has intimated that she wishes me to forget her ? No, I do not."

What a horribly complicated revenge ! thought I, as I said, ever lower and lower, more and more shamefacedly, while the

young violinist sat with the child on his knee,
and his soft brown eyes staring at me in
wonder :

" I think you must remember. You helped
me at Köln, and you paid for my ticket to
Elberthal, and for something that I had at
the hotel. You told me that was what I
owed you."

I again tendered the money ; again he
made no effort to receive it, but said :

" I am sorry that I do not understand to
what you refer. I only know it is impossible that I could ever have told you you
owed me three thalers, or three anything, or
that there could, under any circumstances,
be any question of money between you and
me. Suppose we consider the topic at an
end."

Such a voice of ice, and such a manner, to
chill the boldest heart, I had never yet
encountered. The cool, unspeakable disdain
cut me to the quick.

" You have no right to refuse the money,"
said I desperately. " You have no right to
insult me by—by——" An appropriate
peroration refused itself.

Again the sweet, proud, courteous smile; not only courteous, but courtly; again the icy little bow of the head, which would have done credit to a prince in displeasure, and which yet had the deference due from a gentleman to a lady.

"You will excuse the semblance of rudeness which may appear if I say that if you unfortunately are not of a very decided disposition, I am. It is impossible that I should ever have the slightest intercourse with a lady who has once unequivocally refused my acquaintance. The lady may honour me by changing her mind; I am sorry that I cannot respond. I do not change mine."

"You *must* let us part on equal terms," I reiterated. "It is unjust——"

"Yourself closed all possibility of the faintest attempt at further acquaintance, *mein Fräulein*. The matter is at an end."

"Herr Courvoisier, I——"

"At an end," he repeated calmly, gently, looking at me as he had often looked at me since the night of *Lohengrin*, with a glance that baffled and chilled me.

" I wished to apologise——"

" For what ?" he inquired, with the faintest
possible look of indifferent surprise.

" For my rudeness—my surprise—I——"

" You refer to one evening at the opera.
You exercised your privilege, as a lady, of
closing an acquaintance which you did not
wish to renew. I now exercise mine, as a
gentleman, of saying that I choose to abide
by that decision, now, and always."

I was surprised. Despite my own apologetic frame of mind, I was surprised at his
hardness ; at the narrowness and ungenerosity
which could so determinedly shut the door in
the face of an humble penitent like me. He
must see how I had repented the stupid slip
I had made; he must see how I desired to
atone for it. It was not a slip of the kind
one would name irreparable, and yet he
behaved to me as if I had committed a
crime ; froze me with looks and words. Was
he so self-conscious and so vain that he could
not get over that small slight to his self-con-
sequence, committed in haste and confusion
by an ignorant girl ? Even *then*, even in
that moment I asked myself these questions,

my astonishment being almost as great as my
pain, for it was the very reverse, the *very*
opposite of what I had pictured to myself.
Once let me see him and speak to him, I
had said to myself, and it would be all right;
every lineament of his face, every tone of his
voice, bespoke a frank, generous nature—one
that could forgive. Alas! and alas! this
was the truth!

He had come to the door; he stood by it
now, holding it open, looking at me so courte-
ously, so deferentially, with a manner of
one who had been a gentleman and lived
with gentlemen all his life, but in a way
which at the same time ordered me out as
plainly as possible.

I went to the door. I could no longer
stand under that chilling glance, nor endure
the cool, polished contempt of the manner.
I behaved by no means heroically; neither
flung my head back, nor muttered any defi-
ance, nor in any way proved myself a person
of spirit. All I could do was to look appealingly into his face; to search the bright,
steady eyes, without finding in them any
hint of softening or relenting.

"Will you not take it, *please?*" I asked in
a quivering voice and with trembling lips.

"Impossible, *mein Fräulein*," with the
same chilly little bow as before.

Struggling to repress my tears, I said no
more, but passed out, cut to the heart. The
door was closed gently behind me. I felt as
if it had closed upon a bright belief of my
youth. I leaned for a moment against the
passage wall, and pressed my hand against
my eyes. From within came the sound of a
child's voice, "*Mein Vater*," and the soft,
deep murmur of Eugen's answer; then I
went downstairs and into the open street.

That hated, hateful three thalers ten groschen were still clasped in my hand. What
was I to do with it? Throw it into the
Rhine, and wash it away for ever? Give it
to some one in need? Fling it into the
gutter? Send it him by post? I dismissed that idea for what it was worth. No;
I would obey his prohibition. I would keep
it—those very coins, and when I felt inclined
to be proud and conceited about anything on
my own account, or disposed to put down
superhuman charms to the account of others,

I would go and look at them, and they would preach me eloquent sermons.

As I went into the house, up the stairs to my room, the front door opened again, and Anna Sartorius overtook me.

"I thought you had left the Probe?" said I, staring at her.

"So I had, *Herzchen*," said she, with her usual ambiguous, mocking laugh; "but I was not compelled to come home, like a good little girl, the moment I came out of the *Tonhalle*. I have been visiting a friend. But where have *you* been, for the Probe must have been over for some time? We heard the people go past; indeed, some of them were staying in the house where I was. Did you take a walk in the moonlight?"

"Good-night," said I, too weary and too indifferent even to answer her.

"It must have been a tiring walk; you seem weary, quite *ermüdet*," said she mockingly, and I made no answer.

"A *Hauptprobe* is a dismal thing, after all," she called out to me from the top of the stairs.

From my inmost heart I agreed with her.

CHAPTER VIII.

KAFFEEKLATSCH.

"*Phillis.* I want none o' thy friendship !
Lesbia. Then take my enmity !"

"WHEN a number of ladies meet together to discuss matters of importance, we call it 'Kaffeeklatsch,'" Courvoisier had said to me on that never-forgotten afternoon of my adventure at Köln.

It was my first Kaffeeklatsch which, in a measure, decided my destiny. Hitherto, that is, up to the end of June, I had not been at any entertainment of this kind. At last there came an invitation to Frau Steinmann and to Anna Sartorius, to assist at a "Coffee" of unusual magnitude, and Frau Steinmann suggested that I should go with them and see what it was like. Nothing loath, I consented.

"Bring some work," said Anna Sartorius to me, "or you will find it *langweilig*—slow, I mean."

"Shall we not have some music?"

"Music, yes, the sweetest of all—that of our own tongues. You shall hear every one's candid opinion of every one else—present company always excepted, and you will see what the state of Elberthal society really is—present company still excepted. By a very strange chance the ladies who meet at a Klatsch are always good, pious, virtuous, and, above all, charitable. It is wonderful how well we manage to keep the black sheep out, and have nothing but lambs immaculate."

"Oh don't!"

"Oh, bah! I know the Elberthal *Klatscherei*. It has picked me to pieces many a time. After you have partaken to-day of its coffee and its cakes, it will pick *you* to pieces."

"But," said I, arranging the ruffles of my

very best frock, which I had been told it was *de rigueur* to wear, "I thought women never gossiped so much amongst men."

Fräulein Sartorius laughed loud and long.

"The men! *Du meine Güte!* Men at a Kaffeeklatsch! Show me the one that a man dare even look into, and I'll crown you —and him too—with laurel, and bay, and the wild parsley. A man at a Kaffee—*mag Gott es bewahren!*"

"Oh!" said I, half disappointed, and with a very poor, mean sense of dissatisfaction at having put on my pretty new dress for the first time only for the edification of a number of virulent gossips.

"Men!" she reiterated with a harsh laugh as we walked towards the Goldsteinstrasse, our destination. "Men — no. We despise their company, you see. We only talk about them directly or indirectly from the moment of meeting to that of parting."

"I'm sorry there are no gentlemen," said I, and I was. I felt I looked well.

Arrived at the scene of the Kaffee, we were conducted to a bedroom where we laid aside our hats and mantles. I was standing before the glass, drawing a comb through my up-turned hair, and contemplating with irrepressible satisfaction the delicate lavender hue of my dress, when I suddenly saw reflected behind me the dark, harshly-cut face of Anna Sartorius. She started slightly; then said, with a laugh which had in it something a little forced :

"We are a contrast, aren't we ? Beauty and the Beast, one might almost say. *Na !* *'s schad't nix.*"

I turned away in a little offended pride. Her familiarity annoyed me. What if she were a thousand times cleverer, wittier, better read than I ? I did not like her. A shade crossed her face.

" Is it that you are thoroughly unamiable ?" said she, in a voice which had reproach in it, " or are all English girls so touchy that they receive a compliment upon their good looks as if it were an offence ?"

" I wish you would not talk of my 'good looks' as if I were a dog or a horse !" said I angrily. " I hate to be flattered. I am no beauty, and do not wish to be treated as if I were."

"Do you always hate it?" said she from the window, whither she had turned. "Ach! there goes Herr Courvoisier!"

The name startled me like a sudden report. I made an eager step forward before I had time to recollect myself—then stopped.

"He is not out of sight yet," said she, with a curious look, "if you wish to see him."

I sat down and made no answer. What prompted her to talk in such a manner? Was it a mere coincidence?

"He is a handsome fellow, *nicht wahr?*" she said, still watching me, while I thought Frau Steinmann never would manage to arrange her cap in the style that pleased her. "But a *Taugenichts* all the same," pursued Anna, as I did not speak. "Don't you think so?" she added.

"A *Taugenichts*—I don't know what that is."

"What you call a good-for-nothing."

"Oh."

"*Nicht wahr?*" she persisted.

"I know nothing about it."

"I do. I will tell you all about him sometime."

" I don't wish to know anything about him."

" So !" said she, with a laugh.

Without further word or look I followed Frau Steinmann downstairs.

The lady of the house was seated in the midst of a large concourse of old and young ladies, holding her own with a well-seasoned hardihood in the midst of the awful Babel of tongues. What a noise ! It smote upon and stunned my confounded ear. Our hostess advanced and led me with a wave of the hand into the centre of the room, when she introduced me to about a dozen ladies ; and every one in the room stopped talking and working, and stared at me intently and un-winkingly until my name had been pronounced, after which some continued still to stare at me, and others audibly repeated or attempted to repeat my name, commenting openly upon it. Meanwhile I was conducted to a sofa at the end of the room, and requested in a set phrase, " *Bitte, Fräulein, nehmen Sie Platz auf dem Sofa,*" with which long custom has since made me familiar, to take my seat upon it. I humbly tried to decline the honour, but Anna Sartorius, behind me, whispered :

"Sit down directly, unless you want to be thought an outer barbarian. The place has been kept for you."

Deeply impressed, and very uncomfortable, I sat down. First one and then another came and spoke and talked to me. Their questions and remarks were much in this style :

"Do you like Elberthal? What is your christian name? How old are you? Have you been or are you engaged to be married? They break off engagements in England for a mere trifle, don't they? *Schrecklich!* Did you get your dress in Elberthal? What did it cost the *elle?* Young English ladies wear silk much more than young German ladies. You never go to the theatre on Sunday in England—you are all *pietistisch.* How beautifully you speak our language! Really no foreign accent!" (This repeatedly and un-blushingly, in spite of my most flagrant mistakes, and in the face of my most feeble, halting, and stammering efforts to make myself understood.) "Do you learn music?

singing ? From whom ? Herr von Francius ?
Ach, *so !*" (Pause, while they all look im-
pressively at me. The very name of Von
Francius calls up emotions of no common
order.) " I believe I have seen you at the
Proben to the *Paradise Lost.* Perhaps you
are the lady who is to take the solos ? Yes !
Du lieber Himmel ! What do you think of
Herr von Francius ? Is he not nice ?" (*Nett,*
though, signifies something feminine and
finikin.) · " No ? How odd ! There is no ac-
counting for the tastes of Englishwomen.
Do you know many people in Elberthal ?
No ? *Schade !* No officers ? not Hauptmann
Sachse ?" (with voice growing gradually
shriller), " nor Lieutenant Pieper ? *Not* know
Lieutenant Pieper! *Um Gotteswillen !* What
do you mean ? He *is* so handsome ! such
eyes ! such a moustache ! *Herrgott !* And you
do not know him ? I will tell you something.
When he went off to the autumn manœuvres
at Frankfurt (I have it on good authority),
twenty young ladies went to see him
off."

" *Disgusting !*" I exclaimed, unable to
control my feelings any longer. I saw

Anna Sartorius malignantly smiling as she rocked herself in an American rocking-chair.

"How! disgusting? You are joking. He had dozens of bouquets. All the girls are in love with him. They compelled the photographer to sell them his photograph, and they all believe he is in love with them. I believe Luise Breidenstein will die if he doesn't propose to her."

"They ought to be ashamed of themselves."

"But he is so handsome, so delightful. He dances divinely, and knows such good riddles, and acts—*ach, himmlisch!*"

"But how absurd to make such a fuss of him!" I cried, hot and indignant. "The idea of going on so about a *man!*"

A chorus, a shriek, a Babel of expostulations.

"*Hör 'mal, Thekla!* Fräulein does not know Lieutenant Pieper, and does not think it right to *schwärm* for him."

"The darling! No one can help it who knows him!" said another.

"Let her wait till she does know him,"

said Thekla, a sentimental young woman, pretty in a certain sentimental way, and graceful too—also sentimentally—with the sentiment that lingers about young ladies' albums with leaves of smooth, various-hued note-paper, and about the sonnets which nestle within the same. There was a sudden shriek :

"There he goes! There is the Herr Lieutenant riding by. *Kommen Sie 'mal her, Fräulein!* See him! Judge for yourself!"

A strong hand dragged me, whether I would or no, to the window, and pointed out to me the Herr Lieutenant riding by. An adorable creature in a Hussar uniform; he had pink cheeks and a straight nose, and the loveliest little model of a moustache ever seen; tightly curling black hair, and the dearest little feet and hands imaginable.

" Oh, the dear, handsome, delightful fellow!" cried one enthusiastic young creature, who had scrambled upon a chair in the background and was gazing after him while another, behind me, murmured in tones of emotion :

" Look how he salutes — *divine*, isn't
it ?"

I turned away, smiling an irrepressible
smile. My musician, with his ample traits
and clear, bold eyes, would have looked a
wild, rough, untamable creature by the side
of that wax-doll beauty—that pretty little
being who had just ridden by. I thought I
saw them side by side—Herr Lieutenant
Pieper and Eugen Courvoisier. The latter
would have been as much more imposing than
the former as an oak is more imposing than
a spruce fir—as Gluck than Lortzing. And
could these enthusiastic young ladies have
viewed the two they would have been true
to their lieutenant; so much was certain.
They would have said that the other was a
wild man, who did not cut his hair often
enough, who had large hands, whose collar
was perhaps chosen more with a view to ease
and the free movement of the throat than to
the smallest number of inches within which
it was possible to confine that throat; who
did not wear polished kid boots, and was not
seen off from the station by twenty devoted
admirers of the opposite sex, was not deluged

with bouquets. With a feeling as of something singing at my heart I went back to my place, smiling still.

"See! she is quite charmed with the Herr Lieutenant! Is he not delightful?"

"Oh, very; so is a Dresden china shepherd, but if you let him fall he breaks."

"*Wie komisch!* how odd!" was the universal comment upon my eccentricity. The conversation then wandered off to other military stars, all of whom were *reizend*, *hübsch* or *nett*. So it went on until I got heartily tired of it, and then the ladies discussed their female neighbours, but I leave that branch of the subject to the intelligent reader. It was the old tune with the old variations, which were rattled over in the accustomed manner. I listened, half curious, half appalled, and thought of various speeches made by Anna Sartorius. Whether she were amiable or not, she had certainly a keen insight into the hearts and motives of her fellow-creatures. Perhaps the gift had soured her.

Anna and I walked home alone. Frau Steinmann was, with other elderly ladies of the company, to spend the evening there.

As we walked down the Königsallée—how
well to this day do I remember it! the chest-
nuts were beginning to fade, the road was
dusty, the sun setting gloriously, the people
thronging in crowds—she said suddenly,
quietly, and in a tone of the utmost composure :

" So you don't admire Lieutenant Pieper
so much as Herr Courvoisier ?"

" What do you mean ?" I cried, astonished,
alarmed, and wondering what unlucky chance
led her to talk to me of Eugen.

" I mean what I say ; and for my part I
agree with you—partly. Courvoisier, bad
though he may be, is a man ; the other a
mixture of doll and puppy."

She spoke in a friendly tone ; discursive,
as if inviting confidence and comment on my
part. I was not inclined to give either. I
shrank with morbid nervousness from owning
to any knowledge of Eugen. My pride, nay,
my very self-esteem, bled whenever I thought
of him or heard him mentioned. Above all,
I shrank from the idea of discussing him, or
anything pertaining to him, with Anna Sartorius.

"It will be time for you to agree with me when I give you anything to agree about," said I coldly. "I know nothing of either of the gentlemen, and wish to know nothing.'

There was a pause. Looking up, I found Anna's eyes fixed upon my face, amazed, reproachful. I felt myself blushing fierily. My tongue had led me astray ; I had lied to her : I knew it.

"Do not say you know nothing of *either* of the gentlemen. Herr Courvoisier was your first acquaintance in Elberthal."

"What ?" I cried, with a great leap of the heart, for I felt as if a veil had suddenly been rent away from before my eyes, and I shown a precipice.

"I saw you arrive with Herr Courvoisier," said Anna calmly ; "at least, I saw you come from the platform with him, and he put you into a droschke. And I saw you cut him at the opera ; and I saw you go into his house after the *Generalprobe.* Will you tell me again that you know nothing of him ? I should have thought you too proud to tell lies."

"I wish you would mind your own business," said I, heartily wishing that Anna Sartorius were at the antipodes.

"Listen!" said she very earnestly, and, I remember it now, though I did not heed it then, with wistful kindness. "I do not bear malice—you are so young and inexperienced. I wish you were more friendly, but I care for you too much to be rebuffed by a trifle. I will tell you about Courvoisier."

"Thank you," said I hastily, "I beg you will do no such thing."

"I know his story. I can tell you the truth about him."

"I decline to discuss the subject," said I, thinking of Eugen, and passionately refusing the idea of discussing him, gossiping about him, with any one.

Anna looked surprised; then a look of anger crossed her face.

"You cannot be in earnest," said she.

"I assure you I am. I *wish you would leave me alone*," I said, exasperated beyond endurance.

"You don't wish to know what I can tell you about him?"

"No, I don't. What is more, if you begin

talking to me about him, I will put my fingers in my ears, and leave you."

"*Then you may learn it for yourself,*" said she suddenly, in a voice little more than a whisper. "You shall rue your treatment of me. And when you know the lesson by heart, then you will be sorry."

"You are officious and impertinent," said I, white with ire. "I don't wish for your society, and will say good-evening to you."

With that I turned down a side street leading into the Alléestrasse, and left her.

CHAPTER IX.

So !
Another chapter read ; with doubtful hand
I turn the page ; with doubtful eye I scan
The heading of the next.

FROM that evening Anna let me alone, as I thought, and I was glad of it, nor did I attempt any reconciliation, for the very good reason that I wished for none.

Soon after our dispute I found upon my plate at breakfast, one morning, a letter directed in a bold, though unformed hand, which I recognised as Stella's :

" DEAR MAY,

" I dare say Adelaide will be writing to you, but I will take time by the forelock, so to speak, and give you *my* views on the subject first.

" There is news, strange to say there is some news to tell you. I shall give it without making any remarks. I shall not say whether I think it good, bad, or indifferent. Adelaide is engaged to Sir Peter le Marchant. It was only made known two days ago. Adelaide thinks he is in love with her. What a strange mistake for *her* to make ! She thinks she can do anything with him. Also a monstrous misapprehension on her part. Seriously, May, I am rather uncomfortable about it, or should be, if it were any one else but Adelaide. But she knows so remarkably well what she is about, that perhaps, after all, my fears are needless. And yet—but it is no use speculating about it—I said I wouldn't.

" She is a queer girl. I don't know how she *can* marry Sir Peter, I must say. I suppose he is awfully rich, and Adelaide has always said that poverty was the most horrible thing in the world. I don't know, I'm sure. I should be inclined to say that Sir Peter was the most horrible thing in the world.

Write soon, and tell me what you think about it.

> "Thine, speculatively,
> "Stella Wedderburn."

I did not feel surprise at this letter. Foreboding, grief, shame, I did experience at finding that Adelaide was bent upon her own misery. But then, I reflected, she cannot be very sensible to misery, or she would not be able to go through with such a purpose. I went upstairs to communicate this news to Miss Hallam. Soon the rapid movement of events in my own affairs completely drove thoughts of Adelaide for a time, at least, out of my mind.

Miss Hallam received the information quietly and with a certain contemptuous indifference. I knew she did not like Adelaide, and I spoke of her as seldom as possible.

I took up some work, glancing at the clock, for I expected Von Francius soon to give me my lesson, and Miss Hallam sat still. I had offered to read to her, and she had declined. I glanced at her now and then. I had grown accustomed to that sarcastic, wrinkled, bitter face, and did not dislike it. Indeed, Miss Hallam had given me abundant proofs that, eccentric though she might be, pessimist in theory, merciless upon human nature, which she spoke of in a manner which sometimes absolutely appalled me, yet in fact, in deed, she was a warm-hearted, generous woman. She had dealt bountifully by me, and I knew she loved me, though she never said so.

" May," she presently remarked, " yesterday, when you were out, I saw Dr. Mittendorf."

" Did you, Miss Hallam ?"

" Yes. He says it is useless my remaining here any longer. I shall never see, and an operation might cost me my life ?"

Half stunned, and not yet quite taking in the whole case, I held my work suspended, and looked at her. She went on :

" I knew it would be so when I came. I don't intend to try any more experiments. I shall go home next week."

Now I grasped the truth.

" Go home, Miss Hallam !" I repeated faintly.

"Yes; of course. There is no reason why I should stay, is there?"

"N—no, I suppose not," I admitted; and contrived to stammer out, "and I am very sorry that Dr. Mittendorf thinks you will not be better."

Then I left the room quickly—I could not stay, I was overwhelmed. It was scarcely ten minutes since I had come upstairs to her. I could have thought it was a week.

Outside the room, I stood on the landing with my hand pressed to my forehead, for I felt somewhat bewildered. Stella's letter was still in my hand. As I stood there Anna Sartorius came past.

"*Guten Tag, Fräulein,*" said she, with a mocking kind of good-nature when she had observed me for a few minutes. "What is the matter? Are you ill? Have you had bad news?"

"Good-morning, Fräulein," I answered quietly enough, dropping my hand from my brow.

I went to my room. A maid was there, and the furniture might have stood as a type of chaos. I turned away, and went to the

empty room in which my piano stood, and
where I had my music lessons. I sat down
upon a stool in the middle of the room, folded
my hands in my lap, and endeavoured to
realise what had happened—what was going
to happen. There rang in my head nothing
but the words, " I am going home next
week."

Home again! What a blank yawned before me at the idea! Leave Elberthal—
leave this new life which had just begun to
grow real to me! Leave it—go away ; be
whirled rapidly away back to Skernford—
away from this vivid life, away from—Eugen.
I drew a long breath, as the wretched igno-
minious idea intruded itself, and I knew now
what it was that gave terror to the prospect
before me. My heart quailed and fainted at
the bare idea of such a thing. Not even
Hobson's choice was open to me. There was
no alternative—I must go. I sat still, and
felt myself growing gradually stiller and
graver and colder as I looked mentally to
every side of my horizon, and found it so
bounded—myself shut in so fast.

There was nothing for it but to return

home, and spend the rest of my life at Skern-ford. I was in a mood in which I could smile. I smiled at the idea of myself growing older and older, and this six weeks that I had spent fading back and back into the distance, and the people into whose lives I had had a cursory glance going on their way, and soon forgetting my existence. Truly, Anna! if you were anxious for me to be miserable, this moment, could you know it, should be sweet to you!

My hands clasped themselves more closely upon my lap, and I sat staring at nothing, vaguely, until a shadow before me caused me to look up. Without my knowing it, Von Francius had come in, and was standing by, looking at me.

"Good-morning!" said I, with a vast effort, partially collecting my scattered thoughts.

"Are you ready for your lesson, *mein Fräulein?*"

"N—no. I think, Herr Direktor, I will not take any lesson to-day, if you will excuse it."

"But why? Are you ill?"

"No," said I. "At least—perhaps I want

to accustom myself to do without music-
lessons "

" So ?"

" Yes, and without many other pleasant
things," said I, dryly and decidedly.

" I do not understand," said he, putting
his hat down, and leaning one elbow upon the
piano, whilst his deep eyes fixed themselves
upon my face, and, as usual, began to compel
my secrets from me.

" I am going home," said I.

A quick look of feeling—whether astonishment, regret, or dismay, I should not like to
have said—flashed across his face.

" Have you had bad news ?"

" Yes, very. Miss Hallam returns to England next week."

" But why do you go ? Why not remain
here ?"

" Gladly, if I had any money," I said,
with a dry smile. " But I have none, and
cannot get any."

" You will return to England *now ?* Do
you know what you are giving up ?"

" Obligation has no choice," said I gracefully. " I would give *anything* if I could

stay here, and not go home again." And
with that I burst into tears. I covered my
face with my hands, and all the pent-up
grief and pain of the coming parting
streamed from my eyes. I wept uncon-
trollably.

He did not interrupt my tears for some
time. When he did speak, it was in a very
gentle voice.

"Miss Wedderburn, will you try to com-
pose yourself, and listen to something I have
to say?"

I looked up. I saw his eyes fixed seriously
and kindly upon me, with an expression quite
apart from their usual indifferent coolness—
with the look of one friend to another—with
such a look as I had seen and have since seen
exchanged between Courvoisier and his friend
Helfen.

"See," said he, " I take an interest in you,
Fräulein May. Why should I hesitate to
say so? You are young—you do not know
the extent of your own strength, or of your
own weakness. I do. I will not flatter—it
is not my way—as I think you know."

I smiled. I remembered the plentiful

blame and the scant praise which it had often fallen to my lot to receive from him.

" I am a strict, sarcastic, disagreeable old pedagogue, as you and so many of my other fair pupils consider," he went on, and I looked up in amaze. I knew that so many of his " fair pupils " considered him exactly the reverse.

" It is my business to know whether a voice is good for anything or not. Now yours, with training, will be good for a great deal. Have you the means, or the chance, or the *possibility* of getting that training in England ?"

" No."

" I should like to help you, partly from the regard I have for you, partly for my own sake, because I think you would do me credit."

He paused. I was looking at him with all my senses concentrated upon what he had said. He had been talking round the subject until he saw that he had fairly fixed my attention; then he said, sharply and rapidly :

14— 2

" Fräulein, it lies with you to choose. Will
you go home and stagnate there, or will you
remain here, fight down your difficulties, and
become a worthy artiste ?"

" Can there be any question as to which
I should *like* to do ?" said I, distracted at the
idea of having to give up the prospect he
held out. " But it is impossible. Miss
Hallam alone can decide."

" But if Miss Hallam consented, you would
remain ?"

" Oh ! Herr von Francius ! You should
soon see whether I would remain !"

" *Also !* Miss Hallam *shall* consent. Now
to our singing !"

I stood up. A singular apathy had come
over me ; I felt no longer my old self. I had
a kind of confidence in Von Francius, and
yet—— Despite my recent trouble, I felt
now a lightness and freedom, and a perfect
ability to cast aside all anxieties, and turn to
the business of the moment—my singing.
I had never sung better. Von Francius
condescended to say that I had done well.
Then he rose.

" Now I am going to have a private inter-

view with Miss Hallam," said he, smiling.
" I am always having private interviews with
her, *nicht wahr ?*   Nay, Fräulein May, do not
let your eyes fill with tears.   Have confidence in yourself and your destiny, as I
have."   .

With that he was gone, leaving me to
practise.   How very kind Von Francius was
to me ! I thought—not in the least the kind
of man people called him.   I had great confidence in him—in his will.   I almost believed
that he would know the right thing to say to
Miss Hallam to get her to let me stay ; but
then, suppose she were willing, I had no possible means of support.   Tired of conjecturing
upon a subject upon which I was so utterly
in the dark, I soon ceased that foolish pursuit.   An hour had passed, when I heard
Von Francius' step, which I knew quite well,
come down the stairs.   My heart beat, but I
could not move.

Would he pass, or would he come and
speak to me ?   He paused.   His hand was
on the lock.   That was he, standing before
me, with a slight smile.   He did not look
like a man defeated—but then, *could* he look

like a man defeated? My idea of him was that he held his own way calmly, and that circumstances respectfully bowed to him.

"The day is gained," said he, and paused; but before I could speak he went on:

"Go to Miss Hallam; be kind to her. It is hard for her to part from you, and she has behaved like a Spartan. I felt quite sorry to have to give her so much pain."

Much wondering what could have passed between them, I left Von Francius silently, and sought Miss Hallam.

"Are you there, May?" said she. "What have you been doing all morning?"

"Practising—and having my lesson."

"Practising — and having your lesson— exactly what I have been doing. Practising giving up my own wishes, and taking a lesson in the art of persuasion, by being myself persuaded. Your singing-master is a wonderful man. He has made me act against my principles."

"Miss Hallam——"

"You were in great trouble this morning when you heard you were to leave Elberthal. I knew it instantly. However, you shall not go unless you choose. You shall stay."

Wondering, I held my tongue.

" Herr von Francius has showed me my duty."

"Miss Hallam," said I suddenly, " I will do whatever you wish. After your kindness to me, you have the right to dispose of my doings. I shall be *glad* to do as you wish."

" Well," said she composedly, " I wish you to write a letter to your parents, which I will dictate; of course they must be consulted. Then, if they consent, I intend to provide you with the means of carrying on your studies in Elberthal under Herr von Francius."

I almost gasped. Miss Hallam, who had been a byword in Skernford, and in our own family, for eccentricity and stinginess, was indeed heaping coals of fire upon my head. I tried, weakly and ineffectually, to express my gratitude to her, and at last said :

" You may trust me never to abuse your kindness, Miss Hallam."

" I have trusted you ever since you refused Sir Peter Le Marchant, and were ready to leave your home to get rid of him," said she, with grim humour.

She then told me that she had settled everything with Von Francius, even that I was to remove to different lodgings, more suited for a solitary student than Frau Steinmann's busy house.

"And," she added, "I shall ask Doctor Mittendorf to have an eye to you now and then, and to write to me of how you go on."

I could not find many words in which to thank her. The feeling that I was *not* going, did *not* need to leave it all, filled my heart with a happiness as deep as it was unfounded and unreasonable.

At my next lesson Von Francius spoke to me of the future.

" I want you to be a real student—no play one," said he, " or you will never succeed. And for that reason I told Miss Hallam that you had better leave this house. There are too many distractions. I am going to put you in a very different place."

"Where ? In which part of the town ?"

" Wehrhahn, 39, is the address," said he.

I was not quite sure where that was, but

did not ask further, for I was occupied in helping Miss Hallam, and wished to be with her as much as I could before she left.

The day of parting came, as come it must. Miss Hallam was gone. I had cried, and she had maintained the grim silence which was her only way of expressing emotion.

She was going back home to Skernford, to blindness, now known to be inevitable, to her saddened, joyless life. I was going to remain in Elberthal—for what ? When I look back I ask myself—was I not as blind as she, in truth ?

" In the afternoon of the day of Miss Hallam's departure, I left Frau Steinmann's house. Clara promised to come and see me sometimes. Frau Steinmann kissed me, and called me *liebes Kind.* I got into the cab and directed the driver to go to Wehrhahn, 39. He drove me along one or two streets into the one known as the Schadowstrasse, a long, wide street, in which stood the Tonhalle. A little past that building, round a corner, and he stopped, on the same side of the road.

" Not here !" said I, putting my head out of the window when I saw the window of the curiosity shop exactly opposite. "Not here!"

"Wehrhahn, 39, Fräulein."

"Yes."

"This is it."

I stared around. Yes—on the wall stood in plainly-to-be-read white letters, *Wehrhahn,* and on the door of the house, 39. Yielding to a conviction that it was to be, I murmured "*Kismet,*" and descended from my chariot.

The woman of the house received me civilly. "The young lady for whom the Herr Direktor had taken lodgings? *Schön!* Please to come this way, Fräulein. The room was on the third étage." I followed her upstairs—steep, dark, narrow stairs, like those of the opposite house. The room was a bare-looking, tolerably large one. There was a little closet of a bedroom opening from it—a scrap of carpet upon the floor, and open windows letting in the air. The woman chatted good-naturedly enough.

"So! I hope the room will suit, Fräulein. It is truly not to be called richly furnished, but one doesn't need that when one is a *Sing-student.* I have had many in my time

—ladies and gentlemen too—pupils of Herr
von Francius often. *Na!* what if they did
make a great noise? I have no children—
thank the good God! and one gets used to
the screaming just as one gets used to
everything else." Here she called me to
the window.

"You might have worse prospects than
this, Fräulein, and worse neighbours than
those over the way. See! there is the old
furniture shop where so many of the *Herren
Maler* go, and then there is Herr Duntze,
the landscape painter, and Herr Knoop who
paints *Genrebilder* and does not make much
by it—so a picture of a child with a ravelled
skein of wool, or a little girl making earrings
for herself with bunches of cherries—for
my part I don't see much in them, and
wonder that there are people who will lay
down good hard thalers for them. Then there
is Herr Courvoisier, the *Musiker*—but perhaps you know who he is?"

"Yes," I assented.

"And his little son!" Here she threw up
her hands. "Ach! the poor man! There
are people who speak against him, and every

one knows he and the Herr Direktor are
not the best friends, but *sehen Sie wohl, Fräulein,* the Herr Direktor is well off, settled,
provided for; Herr Courvoisier has his way
to make yet, and the world before him; and
what sort of a story it may be with the
child, I don't know, but this I will say, let
those dare to doubt it or question it who will,
he is a good father—I know it. And the
other young man with Herr Courvoisier—
his friend, I suppose—he is a *Musiker* too.
I hear them practising a good deal sometimes—things without any air or tune to
them: for my part I wonder how they can
go on with it. Give me a good song with a
tune in it—*Drunten im Unterland,* or *In
Berlin, sagt er,* or something one knows. *Na!*
I suppose the fiddling all lies in the way of
business, and perhaps they can fall asleep over
it sometimes, as I do now and then over my
knitting, when I'm weary. The young man,
Herr Courvoisier's friend, looked ill when they
first came; even now he is not to call a robust-
looking person—but formerly he looked as if
he would go out of the fugue altogether.
Entschuldigen, Fräulein, if I use a few pro-

fessional proverbs. My husband, the sainted man! was a piano-tuner by calling, and I have picked up some of his musical expressions and use them, more for his sake than any other reason—for I have heard too much music to believe in it so much as ignorant people do. *Nun!* I will send Fräulein her box up, and then I hope she will feel comfortable and at home, and send for whatever she wants."

In a few moments my luggage had come upstairs, and when they who brought it had finally disappeared, I went to the window again and looked out. Opposite, on the same étage, were two windows, corresponding to my two, wide open, letting me see into an empty room, in which there seemed to be books and many sheets of white paper, a music desk and a vase of flowers. I also saw a piano in the clear-obscure, and another door, half open, leading into the inner room. All the inhabitants of the rooms were out. No tone came across to me—no movement of life. But the influence of the absent ones was there. Strange concourse of circumstances which had placed me as the opposite neighbour, in the same profession too, of Eugen Courvoisier! Pure chance it certainly was, for Von Francius had certainly had no motive in bringing me hither.

" *Kismet !*" I murmured once again, and wondered what the future would bring.

BOOK III.

EUGEN COURVOISIER.

CHAPTER I.

" He looks his angel in the face
  Without a blush : nor heeds disgrace,
  Whom nought disgraceful done
  Disgraces. Who knows nothing base
              Fears nothing known."

I T was noon. The Probe to *Tann-häuser* was over, and we, the members of the *Kapelle*, turned out, and stood in a knot around the orchestra entrance to the Elberthal Theatre.

It was a raw October noontide. The last traces of the bygone summer were being swept away by equinoctial gales, which whirled the remaining yellowing leaves from the trees, and strewed with them the walks of the deserted *Hofgarten* ; a stormy grey sky promised rain at the earliest opportunity; our Rhine went gliding by like a stream of ruffled lead.

"Proper theatre weather," observed one of my fellow-musicians ; "but it doesn't seem to suit you, Friedhelm. What makes you look so down ?"

I shrugged my shoulders. Existence was not at that time very pleasant to me ; my life's hues were somewhat of the colour of the autumn skies and of the dull river. I scarcely knew why I stood with the others now ; it was more a mechanical pause before I took my spiritless way home, than because I felt any interest in what was going on.

"I should say he will be younger by a long way than old Köhler," observed Karl Linders, one of the violoncellists, a young man with an unfailing flow of good-nature, good spirits, and eagerness to enjoy every pleasure which came in his way, which qualities were the objects of my deep wonder

and mild envy. "And they say," he continued, "that he's coming to-night; so Friedhelm, my boy, you may look out. Your
master's on the way."

"So!" said I, lending but an indifferent
attention; "what is his name?"

"That's his way of gently intimating that
he hasn't got no master," said Karl jocosely,
but the general answer to my question was,
"I don't know."

"But they say," said a tall man who
wore spectacles and sat behind me in the
first violins—"they say that Von Francius
doesn't like the appointment. He wanted
some one else, but *Die Direktion* managed to
beat him. He dislikes the new fellow before-
hand, whatever he may be."

"So!—Then he will have a roughish time
of it!" agreed one or two others.

The "he" of whom they spoke was the
coming man who should take the place of
leader of the first violins—it followed that he
would be at least an excellent performer—
possibly a clever man in many other ways,
for the post was in many ways a good one.
Our *Kapelle* was no mean one—in our own

estimation at any rate. Our late first violinist,
who had recently died, had been on visiting
terms with persons of the highest respect-
ability, had given lessons to the very best
families, and might have been seen bowing
to young ladies and important dowagers
almost any day. No wonder his successor
was speculated about with some curiosity.

"*Alle Wetter!*" cried Karl Linders impatiently—that young man was much given
to impatience—"what does Von Francius
want? he can't have everything. I suppose
this new fellow plays a little too well for his
taste. He will have to give him a solo now
and then instead of keeping them all for
himself."

"*Weiss 's nit,*" said another, shrugging his
shoulders; "I've only heard that Von Francius
had a row with the Direction, and was out-
voted."

"What a sweet temper he will be in
at the Probe to-morrow!" laughed Karl.
"Won't he give it to the *Mädchen* right and
left!"

"What time is he coming?" proceeded one
of the oboists.

"Don't know: know nothing about it; perhaps he'll appear in *Tannhäuser* to-night. Look out, Friedhelm."

"Here comes little Luischen," said Karl, with a winning smile, a straightening of his collar, and a general arming-for-conquest expression, as some of the "ladies of the chorus and ballet" appeared from a side door. "Isn't she pretty?" he went on, in an audible aside to me. "I've a crow to pluck with her too. *Tag, Fräulein!*" he added, advancing to the young lady who had so struck him.

He was "struck" on an average once a week, every time with the most beautiful and charming of her sex. The others, with one or two exceptions, also turned. I said good-morning to Linders, who wished, with a noble generosity, to make me a partaker in his cheerful conversation with Fräulein Luise of the first soprans, slipped from his grasp and took my way homewards. Fräulein Luischen was no doubt very pretty, and in her way a companionable person. Unfortunately I never could appreciate that way. With every wish to accommodate myself to the only

society with which fortune supplied me, it
was but ill that I succeeded.

I, Friedhelm Helfen, was at that time a
lonely, soured misanthrope of two and twenty.
Let the announcement sound as absurd as it
may, it is simply and absolutely true. I was
literally alone in the world. My last relative
had died and left me entirely without any one
who could have even a theoretical reason for
taking any interest in me. Gradually during
the last few months, I had fallen into evil
places of thought and imagination. There
had been a time before, as there has been a
time since—as it is with me now—when I
worshipped my art with all my strength as
the most beautiful thing on earth ; the art of
arts—the most beautiful and perfect develop-
ment of beauty which mankind has yet succeeded in attaining to, and when the very
fact of its being so and of my being gifted
with some poor power of expressing and in-
terpreting that beauty was enough for me—
gave me a place in the world with which I
was satisfied, and made life understandable to
me. At that time this belief—my natural
and normal state—was clouded over; between

me and the goddess of my idolatry had fallen
a veil; I wasted my brain tissue in trying to
philosophise—cracked my head, and almost
my reason over the endless, unanswerable
question, *Cui bono?* that question which
may so easily become the destruction of the
fool who once allows himself to be drawn into
dallying with it. *Cui bono?* is a mental
Delilah who will shear the locks of the most
arrogant Samson. And into the arms and
to the tender mercies of this Delilah I had
given myself. I was in a fair way of being
lost for ever in her snares, which she sets for
the feet of men. To what use all this toil?
To what use—*music?* After by dint of
hard twisting my thoughts and coping desperately with problems that I did not
understand, having managed to extract a
conviction that there *was* use in music—a
use to beautify, gladden, and elevate—I
began to ask myself, further: "What
is it to *me* whether mankind is elevated
or not? made better or worse? higher or
lower?"

Only one who has asked himself that
question, as I did, in bitter earnest, and

fairly faced the answer, can know the horror, the blackness, the emptiness of the abyss into which it gives one a glimpse. Blackness of darkness—no standpoint, no vantage-ground —it is a horror of horrors ; it haunted me then day and night, and constituted itself not only my companion but my tyrant.

I was in bad health too. At night, when the joyless day was over, the work done, the play played out, the smell of the footlights and gas and the dust of the stage dispersed, a deadly weariness used to overcome me : an utter, tired, miserable apathy ; and alone, surrounded by loneliness, I let my morbid thoughts carry me whither they would. It had gone so far that I had even begun to say to myself lately :

" Friedhelm Helfen, you are not wanted. On the other side this life is a nothingness so large that you will be as nothing in it. Launch yourself into it. The story that suicide is wrong and immoral is, like other things, to be taken with reservation. There is no absolute right and wrong. Suicide is sometimes the highest form of right and reason."

This mood was strong upon me on that particular day, and as I paced along the Schadowstrasse towards the Wehrhahn, where my lodging was, the very stones seemed to cry out, "The world is weary, and you are not wanted in it."

A heavy, cold, beating rain began to fall. I entered the room which served me as living and sleeping room. From habit I ate and drank at the same restauration as that frequented by my *confrères* of the orchestra. I leaned my elbows upon the table, and listened drearily to the beat of the rain upon the pane. Scattered sheets of music containing, some great, others little thoughts lay around me. Lately it seemed as if the flavour was gone from them. The other night Beethoven himself had failed to move me ; and I accepted it as a sign that all was over with me. In an hour it would be time to go out and seek dinner, if I made up my mind to have any dinner. Then there would be the afternoon—the dreary, wet afternoon, the tramp through the soaking streets, with the lamplight shining into the pools of water, to the theatre ; the lights, the people, the weary round of painted ballet-girls, and accustomed voices and faces of audience and performers. The same number of bars to play, the same to leave unplayed; the whole dreary story, gone through so often before, to be gone through so often again.

The restauration did not see me that day; I remained in the house. There was to be a great concert in the course of a week or two; the "Tower of Babel" was to be given at it. I had the music. I practised my part, and I remember being a little touched with the exquisite loveliness of one of the choruses, that sung by the "Children of Japhet" as they wander sadly away with their punishment upon them into the *Waldeinsamkeit* (that lovely and untranslatable word) one of the purest and most pathetic melodies ever composed.

It was dark that afternoon. I had not stirred from my hole since coming in from the Probe—had neither eaten nor drunk, and was in full possession of the uninterrupted solitude coveted by busy men. Once I thought that it would have been pleasant if some one had known and cared for me well enough to run up the stairs, put his head into the room, and talk to me about his affairs.

To the sound of gustily blowing wind and rain beating on the pane, the afternoon hours dragged slowly by, and the world went on outside and around me until about five o'clock. Then there came a knock at my door, an occurrence so unprecedented that I sat and stared at the said door instead of speaking, as if Edgar Poe's raven had put in a sudden appearance and begun to croak its "never- more" at *me*.

The door was opened. A dreadful, dirty- looking young woman, a servant of the house, stood in the doorway.

"What do you want?" I inquired.

A gentleman wished to speak to me.

"Bring him in then," said I, somewhat testily.

She turned and requested some one to come forward. There entered a tall and stately man, with one of those rare faces, beautiful in feature, bright in expression, which one meets sometimes, and having once seen, never forgets. He carried what I took at first for a bundle done up in a dark green plaid, but as I stood up and looked at him I perceived that the plaid was wrapped round a child. Lost in astonishment I gazed at him in silence.

"I beg you will excuse my intruding upon you thus," said he, bowing, and I involuntarily returned his bow, wondering more and more what he could be. His accent was none of the Elberthal one; it was fine, refined, polished.

"How can I serve you?" I asked, impressed by his voice, manner, and appearance; agreeably impressed. A little masterful he looked—a little imperious, but not unapproachable, with nothing ungenial in his pride.

"You could serve me very much by giving me one or two pieces of information. In the first place let me introduce myself; you, I think, are Herr Helfen?" I bowed. "My name is Eugen Courvoisier. I am the new member of your *städtisches Orchester.*"

"*Oh, was!*" said I, within myself. "*That* our new first violin!"

"And this is my son," he added, looking

down at the plaid bundle, which he held very
carefully and tenderly. " If you will tell me
at what time the opera begins, what it is
to-night, and finally, if there is a room to be
had, perhaps, in this house, even for one night.
I must find a nest for this *Vögelein* as soon as
I possibly can."

" I believe the opera begins at seven," said
I, still gazing at him in astonishment, with
open mouth and incredulous eyes. Our orchestra contained amongst its sufficiently
varied specimens of nationality and appearance, nothing in the very least like this man,
beside whom I felt myself blundering, clumsy,
and unpolished. It was *not* mere natural
grace of manner. He had that, but it had
been cultivated somewhere, and cultivated
highly.

" Yes ?" he said.

" At seven—yes. It is *Tannhäuser* to-
night. And the rooms—I believe they have
rooms in the house."

" Ah, then I will inquire about it," said he,
with an exceedingly open and delightful smile.
" I thank you for telling me. Adieu, *mein
Herr.*"

" Is he asleep ?" I asked abruptly, and pointing to the bundle.

" Yes; *armes Kerlchen!* just now he is," said the young man.

He was quite young, I saw. In that half light I supposed him even younger than he really was. He looked down at the bundle again and smiled.

" I should like to see him," said I politely and gracefully, seized by an impulse of which I felt ashamed, but which I yet could not resist.

With that I stepped forward and came to examine the bundle. He moved the plaid a little aside and showed me a child—a very young, small, helpless child, with closed eyes, immensely long, black, curving lashes, and fine, delicate black brows. The small face was flushed, but even in sleep *this* child looked melancholy. Yet he was a lovely child—most beautiful and most pathetic to see.

I looked at the small face in silence, and a great desire came upon me to look at it oftener —to see it again, then up at that of the father. How unlike the two faces ! Now that I fairly looked at the man I found he was different from what I had thought ; older, sparer, with more sharply-cut features. I could not tell what the child's eyes might be—those of the father were piercing as an eagle's ; clear, open, strange. There was sorrow in the face, I saw, as I looked so earnestly into it ; and it was worn as if with a keen inner life. This glance was one of those which penetrate deep, not the glance of a moment, but a revelation for life.

" He is very beautiful," said I.

" *Nicht wahr ?*" said the other softly.

" Look here," I added, going to a sofa which was strewn with papers, books, and other paraphernalia ; " couldn't we put him here, and then go and see about the rooms ? Such a young, tender child must not be carried about the passages, and the house is full of draughts."

I do not know what had so suddenly supplied me with this wisdom as to what was good for a " young, tender child," nor can I account for the sudden deep interest which possessed me. I dashed the things off the sofa, beat the dust from it, desired him to wait one moment while I rushed to my bed to ravish it of its pillow. Then with the sight of the bed (I was buying my experience) I knew that that, and not the sofa, was the place for the child, and said so.

"Put him here, do put him here!" I besought earnestly. "He will sleep for a time here, won't he?"

"You are very good," said my visitor, hesitating a moment.

"Put him there!" said I, flushed with excitement, and with the hitherto unknown joy of being able to offer hospitality.

Courvoisier looked meditatively at me for a short time, then laid the child upon the bed, and arranged the plaid around it as skilfully and as quickly as a woman would have done it.

"How clever he must be," I thought, looking at him with awe, and with little less awe contemplating the motionless child.

"Wouldn't you like something to put over him?" I asked, looking excitedly about. "I have an overcoat. I'll lend it you." And I was rushing off to fetch it, but he laughingly laid his hand upon my arm.

"Let him alone," said he; "he's all right."

"He won't fall off, will he?" I asked anxiously.

"No; don't be alarmed. Now, if you will be so good, we will see about the rooms."

"Dare you leave him?" I asked, still with anxiety, and looking back as we went towards the door.

"I dare because I must," replied he.

He closed the door, and we went downstairs to seek the persons in authority. Courvoisier related his business and condition, and asked to see rooms. The woman hesitated when she heard there was a child.

"The child will never trouble you, madam," said he quietly, but rather as if the patience of his look were forced.

"No, never!" I added fervently. "I will answer for that, Frau Schmidt."

A quick glance, half gratitude, half amusement, shot from his eyes as the woman went on to say that she only took gentlemen lodgers, and could not do with ladies, children, and nursemaids. They wanted so much attending to, and she did not profess to open her house to them.

" You will not be troubled with either lady or nursemaid," said he. " I take charge of the child myself. You will not know that he is in the house."

" But your wife—" she began.

" There will be no one but myself and my little boy," he replied, ever politely, but ever, as it seemed to me, with repressed pain or irritation.

" So !" said the woman, treating him to a long, curious, unsparing look of wonder and inquiry which made me feel hot all over. He returned the glance quietly, and un-smilingly. After a pause she said :

" Well, I suppose I must see about it, but it will be the first child I ever took into the house in that way, and only as a favour to Herr Helfen."

I was greatly astonished, not having known before that I stood in such high esteem. Courvoisier threw me a smiling glance as we followed the woman up the stairs, up to the top of the house, where I lived. Throwing open a door, she said there were two rooms which must go together. Courvoisier shook his head.

"I do not want two rooms," said he, "or rather, I don't think I can afford them. What do you charge?"

She told him.

"If it were so much," said he, naming a smaller sum, "I could do it."

"*Nee!*" said the woman curtly; "for that I can't do it. *Um Gotteswillen!* One must live."

She paused, reflecting, and I watched anxiously. She was going to refuse. My heart sank. Rapidly reviewing my own circumstances and finances, and making a hasty calculation in my mind, I said:

"Why can't we arrange it? Here is a big room and a little room. Make the little room into a bedroom, and use the big room for a sitting-room. I will join at it, and so it will come within the price you wish to pay."

The woman's face cleared a little. She had listened with a clouded expression and her head on one side. Now she straightened herself, drew herself up, smoothed down her apron, and said :

"Yes, that lets itself be heard. If Herr Helfen agreed to that, she would like it."

"Oh, but I can't think of putting you to the extra expense," said Courvoisier.

"I should like it," said I. "I have often wished I had a little more room, but, like you, I couldn't afford the whole expense. We can have a piano, and the child can play there. Don't you see?" I added, with great earnestness and touching his arm. "It is a large airy room; he can run about there, and make as much noise as he likes."

He still seemed to hesitate.

"I can afford it," said I. "I've no one but myself, unluckily. If you don't object to my company, let us try it. We shall be neighbours in the orchestra."

"So!"

"Why not at home too? I think it is an excellent plan. Let us decide it so."

I was very urgent about it. An hour ago I could not have conceived anything which could make me so urgent and set my heart beating so.

" If I did not think it would inconvenience you," he began.

" Then it is settled ?" said I. " Now let us go and see what kind of furniture there is in that big room."

Without allowing him to utter any further objection I dragged him to the large room, and we surveyed it. The woman, who for some unaccountable reason appeared to have recovered her good temper in a marvellous manner, said quite cheerfully that she would send the maid to make the smaller room ready as a bedroom for two. " One of us won't take much room," said Courvoisier with a laugh, to which she assented with a smile, and then left us. The big room was long, low, and rather dark. Beams were across the ceiling, and two not very large windows looked upon the street below, across to two similar windows of another lodging-house ; a little to the left of which was the Tonhalle. The floor was carpetless, but clean ; there was a big square table, and some chairs.

" There," said I, drawing Courvoisier to the window, and pointing across ; " there is

16—2

one scene of your future exertions, the *Städtische Tonhalle.*"

"So!" said he, turning away again from the window : it was as dark as ever outside, and looking round the room again. "This is a dull-looking place," he added, gazing around it.

"We'll soon make it different," said I, rubbing my hands and gazing round the room with avidity. "I have long wished to be able to inhabit this room. We must make it more cheerful, though, before the child comes to it. We'll have the stove lighted, and we'll knock up some shelves, and we'll have a piano in, and the sofa from my room, *nicht wahr?* Oh, we'll make a place of it, I can tell you."

He looked at me as if struck with my enthusiasm, and I bustled about. We set to work to make the room habitable. He was out for a short time at the station, and returned with the luggage which he had left there. While he was away I stole into my room and took a good look at my new treasure ; he still slept peacefully and calmly on. We were deep in *impromptu* carpentering

and contrivances for use and comfort, when it
occurred to me to look at my watch.

" Five minutes to seven !" I almost yelled,
dashing wildly into my room to wash my
hands and get my violin. Courvoisier followed me. The child was awake. I felt a
horrible sense of guilt as I saw it looking at
me with great, soft, solemn, brown eyes, not
in the least those of its father, but it did not
move. I said apologetically that I feared I
had wakened it.

" Oh no ! He's been awake for some
time," said Courvoisier. The child saw him,
and stretched out its arms towards him.

" *Na! junger Taugenichts!*" he said, taking
it up and kissing it. " Thou must stay
here till I come back. Wilt be happy till I
come ?"

The answer made by the mournful-looking
child was a singular one. It put both tiny
arms around the big man's neck, laid its face
for a moment against his, and loosed him
again. Neither word nor sound did it emit
during the process. A feeling altogether
new and astonishing overcame me. I turned
hastily away, and as I picked up my violin-

case, was amazed to find my eyes dim. My
visitors were something unprecedented to
me.

" You are not compelled to go to the
theatre to-night, you know, unless you like,"
I suggested, as we went downstairs.

" Thanks, it is as well to begin at once."

On the lowest landing we met Frau
Schmidt.

" Where are you going, *meine Herren?*"
she demanded.

" To work, madame," he replied, lifting his
cap with a courtesy which seemed to disarm
her.

" But the child ?" she demanded.

" Do not trouble yourself about him."

" Is he asleep ?"

" Not just now. He is all right, though."

She gave us a look which meant volumes.
I pulled Courvoisier out.

" Come along, do !" cried I. " She will
keep you there for half an hour, and it is
time now."

We rushed along the streets too rapidly to
have time or breath to speak, and it was five
minutes after the time when we scrambled

into the orchestra, and found that the overture was already begun.

Though there is certainly not much time
for observing one's fellows when one is helping in the overture to *Tannhäuser*, yet I saw
the many curious and astonished glances
which were cast towards our new member,
glances of which he took no notice, simply
because he apparently did not see them. He
had the finest absence of self-consciousness
that I ever saw.

The first act of the opera was over, and
it fell to my share to make Courvoisier known
to his fellow-musicians. I introduced him to
the Director, who was not Von Francius, nor
any friend of his. Then we retired to one of
the small rooms on one side of the orchestra.

"*Hundewetter!*" said one of the men,
shivering. " Have you travelled far to
day ?" he inquired of Courvoisier, by way of
opening the conversation.

" From Köln only."

" Live there ?"

" No."

The man continued his catechism, but in
another direction.

" Are you a friend of Helfen's ?"

" I rather think Helfen has been a friend to me," said Courvoisier, smiling.

" Have you found lodgings already ?"

" Yes."

" So !" said his interlocutor, rather puzzled with the new arrival. I remember the scene well. Half-a-dozen of the men were standing in one corner of the room, smoking, drinking beer, and laughing over some not very brilliant joke ; we three were a little apart. Courvoisier stately and imposing-looking, and with that fine manner of his, politely answering his interrogator, a small, sharp-featured man, who looked up to him, and rattled complacently away, while I sat upon the table amongst the fiddle-cases and beer-glasses, my foot on a chair, my chin in my hand, feeling my cheeks glow, and a strange sense of dizziness and weakness all over me, a lightness in my head which I could not understand. It had quite escaped me that I had neither eaten nor drunk since my break-fast at eight o'clock, on a cup of coffee and a dry *Brödchen,* and it was now twelve hours later.

The pause was not a long one, and we returned to our places. But *Tannhäuser* is not a short opera. As time went on my sensations of illness and faintness increased. During the second pause I remained in my place. Courvoisier presently came and sat beside me.

" I'm afraid you feel ill," said he.

I denied it. But though I struggled on to the end, yet at last a deadly faintness overcame me. As the curtain went down amidst applause, everything reeled around me. I heard the bustle of the others—of the audience going away. I myself could not move.

" *Was ist denn mit ihm ?*" I heard Courvoisier say as he stooped over me.

" Is that Friedhelm Helfen?" asked Karl Linders, surveying me. " *Potz blitz !* he looks like a corpse ! he's been at his old tricks again, starving himself. I expect he has touched nothing the whole day."

" Let's get him out and give him some brandy," said Courvoisier. " Lend him an arm, and I'll give him one on this side."

Together they hauled me down to the retiring-room.

" *Ei!* he wants a Schnapps, or something of the kind," said Karl, who seemed to think the whole affair an excellent joke. " Look here, *alter Narr!*" he added ; " you've been going without anything to eat, *nicht?*"

" I believe I have," I assented feebly. " But I'm all right ; I'll go home."

Rejecting Karl's pressing entreaties to join him at supper at his favourite *Wirthschaft*, we went home, purchasing our supper on the way. Courvoisier's first step was towards the place where he had left the child. He was gone.

" *Verschwunden!*" cried he, striding off to the sleeping-room, whither I followed him. The little lad had been undressed and put to bed in a small crib, and was sleeping serenely.

" That's Frau Schmidt, who can't do with children and nursemaids," said I, laughing.

" It's very kind of her," said he, as he touched the child's cheek slightly with his little finger, and then, without another word, returned to the other room, and we sat down to our long-delayed supper.

"What on earth made you spend more than twelve hours without food?" he asked me, laying down his knife and fork, and looking at me.

"I'll tell you some time perhaps, not now," said I, for there had begun to dawn upon my mind, like a sun-ray, the idea that life held an interest for me—two interests—a friend and a child. To a miserable, lonely wretch like me, the idea was divine.

CHAPTER II.

"Though nothing can bring back the hour
  Of splendour in the grass, of glory in the flower,
We will grieve not—rather find
Strength in what remains behind;
In the primal sympathy
Which, having been, must ever be.
In the soothing thoughts that spring
Out of human suffering!
In the faith that looks through death—
In years, that bring the philosophic mind."

WORDSWORTH.

FROM that October afternoon I
was a man saved from myself.
Courvoisier had said, in answer to
my earnest entreaties about joining house-
keeping: "We will try—you may not like
it, and if so, remember you are at liberty to
withdraw when you will." The answer con-

tented me, because I knew that I should not try to withdraw.

Our friendship progressed by such quiet, imperceptible degrees, each one knotting the past more closely and inextricably with the present, that I could by no means relate them if I wished it. But I do not wish it. I only know, and am content with it, that it has fallen to my lot to be blessed with that most precious of *all* earthly possessions, the "friend" that "sticketh closer than a brother." Our union has grown and remained not merely *"fest und treu,"* but immovable, unshakable.

There was first the child. He was two years old : a strange, weird, silent child, very beautiful—as the son of his father could scarcely fail to be—but with a different kind of beauty. How still he was, and how patient ! Not a fretful child, not given to crying or complaint ; fond of resting in one place, with solemn, thoughtful eyes fixed, when his father was there, upon him ; when his father was not there, upon the strip of sky which was to be seen through the window above the house-tops.

The child's name was Sigmund; he displayed a friendly disposition towards me, indeed he was passively friendly and—if one may say such a thing of a baby—courteous to all he came in contact with. He had inherited his father's polished manner; one saw that when he grew up he would be a " gentleman," in the finest outer sense of the word. His inner life he kept concealed from us. I believe he had some method of communicating his ideas to Eugen, even if he never spoke. Eugen could never conceal his own mood from the child; it knew—let him feign otherwise never so cunningly—exactly what he felt, glad or sad, or between the two, and no acting could deceive him. It was a strange, intensely interesting study to me; one to which I daily returned with fresh avidity. He would let me take him in my arms and talk to him; would sometimes, after looking at me long and earnestly, break into a smile—a strange, grave, sweet smile. Then I could do no otherwise than set him hastily down, and look away, for so unearthly a smile I had never seen. He was, though fragile, not an unhealthy child; though so delicately formed, and intensely sensitive to nervous shocks, had nothing of the coward in him, as was proved to us in a thousand ways : shivered through and through his little frame at the sight of a certain picture to which he had taken a great antipathy, a picture which hung in the public gallery at the Tonhalle : he hated it, because of a certain evil-looking man portrayed in it ; but when his father, taking his hand, said to him, " Go, Sigmund, and look at that man ; I wish thee to look at him," went, without turn or waver, and gazed long and earnestly at the low-type, bestial visage portrayed to him. Eugen had trodden noiselessly behind him ; I watched, and he watched, how his two little fists clenched themselves at his sides, while his gaze never wavered, never wandered, till at last Eugen, with a strange expression, caught him in his arms and half killed him with kisses.

" *Mein Liebling !*" he murmured, as if utterly satisfied with him.

Courvoisier himself ? There were a great many strong and positive qualities about this man, which in themselves would have set him somewhat apart from other men. Thus he had crotchety ideas about truth and honour, such as one might expect from so knightly-looking a personage. It was Karl Linders who, at a later period of our acquaintance, amused himself by chalking up, "*Prinz Eugen, der edle Ritter,*" beneath his name. His musical talent—or rather genius, it was more than talent—was at that time not one-fifth part known to me, yet even what I saw excited my wonder. But these, and a long list of other active characteristics, all faded into insignificance before the towering passion of his existence—his love for his child. It was strange, it was touching, to see the bond between father and son. The child's thoughts and words, as told in his eyes and from his lips, formed the man's philosophy. I believe Eugen confided everything to his boy. His first thought in the morning, his last at night, was for *der Kleine.* His leisure was—I cannot say "given up" to the boy—but it was always passed with him.

Courvoisier soon gained a reputation among our comrades for being a sham and a delusion. They said that to look at him one would suppose that no more genial, jovial fellow could exist—there was kindliness in his glance, *bon camaraderie* in his voice, a genial, open, human, sympathetic kind of influence in his nature, and in all he did, "And yet," said Karl Linders to me, with gesticulation, "one never can get him to go anywhere. One may invite him, one may try to be friends with him, but, no! off he goes *home!* What does the fellow want at home? He behaves like a young miss of fifteen, whose governess won't let her mix with vulgar companions."

I laughed, despite myself, at this tirade of Karl. So that was how Eugen's behaviour struck outsiders!

"And you are every bit as bad as he is, and as soft—he has made you so," went on Linders vehemently. "It isn't right. You two ought to be the leaders outside as well as in, but you walk yourselves away, and stay at *home!* At home, indeed! Let green goslings and grandfathers stay at home."

Indeed, Herr Linders was not a person who troubled home much; spending his time from morning to night between theatre and concert-room, restauration and *Verein.*

"What do you *do* at home?" he asked irately.

"That's our concern, *mein Lieber*," said I composedly, thinking of young Sigmund, whose existence was unknown except to our two selves, and laughing.

"Are you composing a symphonie? or an opera buffa? You might tell a fellow."

I laughed again, and said we led a peaceable life, as honest citizens should; and added, laying my hand upon his shoulder, for I had more of a leaning towards Karl, scamp though he was, than to any of the others, "You might do worse than follow our example, old fellow."

"Bah!" said he, with unutterable contempt. "I'm a man; not a milksop. Besides, how do I know what your example is? You *say* you behave yourselves; but how am I to know it? I'll drop upon you unawares, and catch you, sometime. See if I don't."

The next evening, by a rare chance with us, was a free one—there was no opera and no concert; we had had Probe that morning, and were at liberty to follow the devices and desires of our own hearts that evening.

These devices and desires led us straight home, followed by a sneering laugh from Herr Linders, which vastly amused me. The year was drawing to a close. Christmas was nigh : the weather was cold and unfriendly. Our stove was lighted ; our lamp burnt pleasantly on the table ; our big room looked homely and charming by these evening lights. Master Sigmund was wide awake in honour of the occasion, and sat upon my knee whilst his father played the fiddle. I have not spoken of his playing before—it was, in its way, unique. It was not a violin that he played—it was a spirit that he invoked—and a strange answer it sometimes gave forth to his summons. To-night he had taken it up suddenly, and sat playing, without book, a strange melody which wrung my heart—full of minor cadences, with an infinite wail and weariness in it. I closed my eyes and listened. It was sad, but it was absorbing. When I opened my eyes again and looked down, I found that tears were running from Sigmund's eyes. He was sobbing quietly— his head against my breast.

"I say, Eugen ! Look here !"

"Is he crying? Poor little chap! He'll have a good deal to go through before he's *fertig mit Allen*," said Eugen, laying down his violin.

"What was that? I never heard it before."

"I have, often," said he, resting his chin upon his hand, "in the sound of streams—in the rush of a crowd—upon a mountain—yes, even alone with the woman I——" he broke off abruptly.

"But never on a violin before?" said I significantly.

"No, never."

"Why don't you print some of those impromptus that you are always making?" I asked.

He shrugged his shoulders. Ere I could pursue the question some one knocked at the door, and in answer to our *Herein!* appeared a handsome, laughing face, and a head of wavy hair, which, with a tall, shapely figure, I recognised as those of Karl Linders.

"I told you fellows I'd hunt you up, and I always keep my word," said he composedly. "You can't very well turn me out for calling upon you."

He advanced. Courvoisier rose, and with a courteous cordiality offered his hand, and drew a chair up. Karl came forward, looking round, smiling and chuckling at the success of his experiment, and as he came opposite to me his eyes fell upon those of the child, who had raised his head and was staring gravely at him.

Never shall I forget the start—the look of amaze, almost of fear, which shot across the face of Herr Linders. Amazement would be a weak word in which to describe it. He stopped, stood stock-still, in the middle of the room ; his jaw fell—he gazed from one to the other of us in feeble astonishment, then said in a whisper :

" *Donnerwetter !* A child !"

" Don't use bad language before the little innocent," said I, enjoying his confusion.

" Which of you does it belong to ?" Is it he or she ?" he inquired in an awe-struck and alarmed manner.

" His name is Sigmund Courvoisier," said I, with difficulty preserving my gravity.

" Oh, indeed ! I—I wasn't aware—" began Karl, looking at Eugen in such a peculiar manner—half respectful, half timid, half

ashamed—that I could no longer contain my
feelings, but burst into such a shout of
laughter as I had not enjoyed for years.
After a moment, Eugen joined in; we
laughed peal after peal of laughter, while
poor Karl stood feebly looking from one to
the other of the company—speechless—crest-
fallen.

" I beg your pardon," he said at last, " I
won't intrude any longer. Good——"

He was making for the door, but Eugen
made a dash after him, turned him round,
and pushed him into a chair.

" Sit down, man," said he, stifling his
laughter. " Sit down, man; do you think
the poor little chap will hurt you ?"

Karl cast a distrustful glance sideways at
my nursling and spoke not.

" I'm glad to see you," pursued Eugen.
" Why didn't you come before ?"

At that Karl's lips began to twitch with a
humorous smile : presently he too began to
laugh, and seemed not to know how or when
to stop.

" It beats all I ever saw or heard or dreamt
of," said he at last. " *That's* what brought

you home in such a hurry every night. Let
me congratulate you, Friedel! You make a
first-rate nurse; when everything else fails
I will give you a character as *Kindermädchen;*
clean, sober, industrious, and not given to running after young men." With which he
roared again, and Sigmund surveyed him
with a somewhat severe, though scarcely a
disapproving expression. Karl seated himself near him, and, though not yet venturing to
address him, cast various glances of blandish-
ment and persuasion upon him.

Half an hour passed thus, and a second
knock was followed by the entrance of Frau
Schmidt.

" Good-evening, gentlemen," she remarked
in a tone which said unutterable things—
scorn, contempt, pity—all finely blended into
a withering sneer, as she cast her eyes around,
and a slight but awful smile played about her
lips. " Half-past eight, and that blessed baby
not in bed yet. I knew how it would be.
And you all smoking, too—*natürlich!* You
ought to know better, Herr Courvoisier—*you*
ought, at any rate," she added, scorn dropping into heart-piercing reproach. " Give

him to me," she added, taking him from me,
and apostrophising him. "You poor, blessed
lamb! Well for you that I'm here to look
after you, that have had children of my own,
and know a *little* about the sort of way that
you ought to be brought up in."

Evident signs of uneasiness on Karl's part,
as Frau Schmidt, with the same extraordinary
contortion of the mouth—half smile, half sneer
—brought Sigmund to his father, to say good-
night. That process over, he was brought to
me, and then, as if it were a matter which
"understood itself," to Karl. Eugen and I, like
family men as we were, had gone through the
ceremony with willing grace. Karl backed
his chair a little, looked much alarmed, shot
a queer glance at us, at the child, and then
appealingly up into the woman's face. We,
through our smoke, watched him.

"He looks so very — very ——" he began.

"Come, come, *mein Herr*, what does that
mean? Kiss the little angel, and be thankful you may. The innocent! You ought to
be delighted," said she, standing with grena-
dier-like stiffness beside him.

"He won't bite you, Karl," I said, reas-
suringly. "He's quite harmless."

Thus encouraged, Herr Linders stooped
forward, and touched the cheek of the child
with his lips; then, as if surprised, stroked
it with his finger.

"*Lieber Himmel!* how soft! Like satin,
or rose-leaves!" he murmured, as the woman
carried the child away, shut the door, and
disappeared.

"Does she tackle you in that way every
night?" he inquired next.

"Every evening," said Eugen. "And I
little dare open my lips before her. You
would notice how quiet I kept. It's because
I am afraid of her."

Frau Schmidt, who had at first objected so
strongly to the advent of the child, was now
devoted to it, and would have resented exceedingly the idea of allowing any one but
herself to put it to bed, dress or undress it,
or look after it in general. This state of
things had crept on very gradually: she had
never *said* how fond she was of the child, but
put her kindness upon the ground that as a
Christian woman she could not stand by and

see it mis-handled by a couple of *men*, and oh! the unutterable contempt upon the word "men." Under this disguise she attempted to cover the fact that she delighted to have it with her, to kiss it, fondle it, admire it, and "do for it." We knew now that no sooner had we left the house than the child would be brought down, and would never leave the care of Frau Schmidt until our return, or until he was in bed and asleep. She said he was a quiet child, and "did not give so much trouble." Indeed the little fellow won a friend in whoever saw him. He had made another conquest to-night. Karl Linders, after puffing away for some time, inquired, with an affectation of indifference:

"How old is he—*der kleine Bengel?*"

"Two—a little more."

"Handsome little fellow!"

"Glad you think so."

"Sure of it. But I didn't know, Courvoisier—so sure as I live, I knew nothing about it!"

"I dare say not. Did I ever say you did?"

I saw that Karl wished to ask another question; one which had trembled upon my own lips many a time, but which I had never asked—which I knew that I never should ask. "The mother of that child—is she alive or dead? Why may we never hear one word of her? Why this silence, as of the grave? Was she your wife? Did you love her? Did she love you?"

Questions which could not fail to come to me, and about which my thoughts would hang for hours. I could imagine a woman being very deeply in love with Courvoisier. Whether he would love very deeply himself, whether love would form a mainspring of his life and actions, or whether it took only a secondary place—I speak of the love of woman—I could not guess. I could decide upon many points of his character. He was a good friend, a high-minded and a pure-minded man; his every-day life, the turn of his thoughts and conversation, showed me that as plainly as any great adventure could have done. That he was an ardent musician, an artist in the truest and deepest sense, of a quixotically generous and unselfish nature— all this I had already proved. That he loved his child with a love not short of passion was patent to me every day. But upon the past, silence so utter as I never before met with. Not a hint; not an allusion; not one syllable.

Little Sigmund was not yet two and a half. The story upon which his father maintained so deep a silence was not, could not be a very old one. His behaviour gave me no clue as to whether it had been a joyful or a sorrowful one. Mere silence could tell me nothing. Some men are silent about their griefs; some about their joys. I knew not in which direction his disposition lay.

I saw Karl look at him that evening once or twice, and I trembled lest the blundering, good-natured fellow should make the mistake of asking some question. But he did not; I need not have feared. People were not in the habit of putting obtrusive questions to Eugen Courvoisier. The danger was somehow quietly tided over, the delicate ground avoided.

The conversation wandered quietly off to common-place topics—the state of the orchestra; tales of its doings; the tempers of our different conductors—Malperg of the opera; Woelfl of the ordinary concerts, which took place two

or three times a week, when we fiddled and
the public ate, drank, and listened ; lastly,
Von Francius, *königlicher Musikdirektor.*

Karl Linders gave his opinion freely upon
the men in authority. He had nothing to do
with them, nothing to hope or fear from them;
he filled a quiet place amongst the violoncellists, and had attained his twenty-eighth
year without displaying any violent talent or
tendency to distinguish himself, otherwise
than by getting as much mirth out of life as
possible, and living in a perpetual state of
" carelesse contente."

He desired to know what Courvoisier
thought of Von Francius ; for curiosity—the
fault of those idle persons who afterwards
develop into busybodies—was already beginning to leave its traces on Herr Linders.
It was less known than guessed that the
state of things between Courvoisier and Von
Francius was less peace than armed neutrality.
The intense politeness of Von Francius to his
first violinist, and the punctilious ceremonious-
ness of the latter towards his chief, were
topics of speculation and amusement to the
whole orchestra.

"I think Von Francius would be a fiend if he could," said Karl comfortably. "I wouldn't stand it if he spoke to me as he speaks to some people."

"Oh, they like it!" said Courvoisier; and Karl stared.

"Girls don't object to a little bullying; anything rather than be left quite alone," he went on tranquilly.

"Girls!" ejaculated Karl.

"You mean the young ladies in the chorus, don't you?" asked Courvoisier, unmovedly. "He *does* bully them, I don't deny; but they come back again."

"Oh, I see!" said Karl, accepting the rebuff.

He had *not* referred to the young ladies of the chorus.

"Have you heard Von Francius play?" he began next.

"*Natürlich!*"

"What do you think of it?"

"I think it is superb!" said Courvoisier.

Baffled again, Karl was silent.

"The power and the daring of it are grand," went on Eugen heartily. "I could listen to him for hours. To see him seat himself before the piano, as if he were sitting down to read a newspaper, and do what he does, without moving a muscle, is simply superb—there's no other word. Other men may play the piano ; he takes the key-board and plays *with* it, and it says what he likes."

I looked at him, and was satisfied. He found the same want in Von Francius's "superb" manipulation that I did—the glitter of a diamond, not the glow of a fire.

Karl had not the subtlety to retort, " Ay, but does it say what *we* like ?" He subsided again, merely giving a meek assent to the proposition, and saying suggestively :

" He's not liked, though he is such a popular fellow."

" The public is often a great fool."

" Well, but you can't expect it to kiss the hand that slaps it in the face, as Von Francius does," said Karl, driven to metaphor, probably for the first time in his life, and seeming astonished at having discovered a hitherto unknown mental property pertaining to himself.

Courvoisier laughed.

"I'm certain of one thing : Von Francius will go on slapping the public's face. I won't say how it will end ; but it would not surprise me in the least to see the public at his feet, as it is now at those of——"

"Humph !" said Karl reflectively.

He did not stay much longer, but having finished his cigar, rose. He seemed to feel very apologetic, and out of the fulness of his heart his mouth spake :

"I really wouldn't have intruded if I had known——"

"Known what ?" inquired Eugen, with well-assumed surprise.

"I thought you were just by yourselves, you know, and——"

"So we are ; but we can do with other society. Friedel here gets very tedious sometimes—in fact, *langweilig.* Come again, *nicht wahr ?*"

"If I shan't be in your way," said Karl, looking round the room with somewhat wistful eyes.

We assured him to the contrary, and he promised, with unnecessary emphasis, to come again.

" He will return ; I know he will !" sang
Eugen after he had gone.

The next time that Herr Linders arrived,
which was ere many days had passed, he
looked excited and important ; and after the
first greetings were over, he undid a great
number of papers, which wrapped and en-
folded a parcel of considerable dimensions,
and displayed to our enraptured view a white
woolly animal of stupendous dimensions, fastened upon a green stand, which stand, when
pressed, caused the creature to give forth a
howl, like unto no lowing of oxen nor bleat-
ing of sheep ever heard on earth. This
inviting-looking creature he held forth towards Sigmund, who stared at it.

" Perhaps he's got one already ?" said
Karl, seeing that the child did not display
any violent enthusiasm about the treasure.

" Oh no !" said Eugen promptly.

" Perhaps he doesn't know what it is," I
suggested rather unkindly, scarcely able to
keep my countenance at the idea of *that* baby
playing with such a toy.

" Perhaps not," said Karl more cheerfully,
kneeling down by my side—Sigmund sat on

my knee—and squeezing the stand, so that the woolly animal howled. "*Sieh!* Sigmund! Look at the pretty lamb!"

"Oh, come, Karl! Are you a lamb? Call it an eagle at once," said I sceptically.

"It *is* a lamb, isn't it?" said he, turning it over. "They called it a lamb at the shop."

"A very queer lamb: not a German breed, anyhow."

"Now I think of it, my little sister has one, but she calls it a rabbit, I believe."

"Very likely. You might call that anything, and no one could contradict you."

"Well, *der Kleine* doesn't know the difference: it's a *toy*," said Karl desperately.

"Not a toy that seems to take his fancy much," said I, as Sigmund, with evident signs of displeasure, turned away from the animal on the green stand, and refused to look at it. Karl looked despondent.

"He doesn't like the look of it," said he plaintively. "I thought I was sure to be right in this. My little sister" (Karl's little sister had certainly never been so often quoted by her brother before) "plays for hours with that thing that she calls a rabbit."

Eugen had come to the rescue, and grasped the woolly animal which Karl had contemptuously thrown aside. After convincing himself by near examination as to which was intended for head, and which for tail, he presented it to his son, remarking that it was " a pretty toy."

" I'll pray for you after that, Eugen—often, and earnestly," said I.

Sigmund looked appealingly at him, but seeing that his father appeared able to endure the presence of the beast, and seemed to wish him to do the same, from some dark and inscrutable reason not to be grasped by so young a mind—for he was modest as to his own intelligence—he put out his small arm, received the creature into it, and embracing it round the body, held it to his side, and looked at Eugen with a pathetic expression.

" Pretty plaything, *nicht wahr ?*" said Eugen encouragingly.

Sigmund nodded, silently. The animal emitted a howl; the child winced, but looked resigned. Eugen rose and stood at some little distance, looking on. Sigmund continued to embrace the animal with the same resigned expression, until Karl, stooping, took it away.

"You mustn't *make* him, just because I brought it," said he. "Better luck next time. I see he's not a common child. I must try to think of something else."

We commanded our countenances with difficulty, but preserved them. Sigmund's feelings had been severely wounded. For many days he eyed Karl with a strange, cold glance, which the latter used every art in his power to change, and at last succeeded. Woolly lambs became a forbidden subject. Nothing annoyed Karl more than for us to suggest, if Sigmund happened to be a little cross or mournful—"Suppose you just go home, Karl, and fetch that 'lamb-rabbit-lion.' I'm sure he would like it." From that time the child had another worshipper, and we a constant visitor in Karl Linders.

We sat together one evening—Eugen and I, after Sigmund had been in bed a long time, after the opera was over—chatting, as we often did, or as often remained silent. He had been reading, and the book from which he read was a volume of English poetry. At last, laying the book aside, he said :

"The first night we met you fainted away from exhaustion and long fasting. You said you would tell me why you had allowed yourself to do so, but you have never kept your word."

"I didn't care to eat. People eat to live— except those who live to eat, and I was not very anxious to live, I didn't care for my life, in fact, I wished I was dead."

"Why ? An unlucky love ?"

"*I, bewahre !* I never knew what it was to be in love in my life," said I, with perfect truth.

"Is that true, Friedel ?" he asked, apparently surprised.

"As true as possible. I think a timely love affair, however unlucky, would have roused me and brought me to my senses again."

"General melancholy ?"

"Oh, I was alone in the world. I had

been reading, reading, reading : my brain was one dark and misty muddle of Kant, Schopenhauer, Von Hartmann, and a few others. I read them one after another, as quickly as possible : the mixture had the same effect upon my mind as the indiscriminate contents of a toffy-shop would have upon Sigmund's stomach—it made it sick. In my crude, ungainly, unfinished fashion I turned over my information, laying down big generalisations upon a foundation of experience of the smallest possible dimensions, and all upon one side."

He nodded. " Ei ! I know it."

" And after considering the state of the human race—that is to say the half dozen people I knew, and the miseries of the human lot as set forth in the books I had read, and having proved to myself, all up in that little room, you know "—I pointed to my bedroom —" that there neither was nor could be heaven or hell or any future state, and having decided, also from that room, that there was no place for me in the world, and that I was very likely actually filling the place of some other man, poorer than I was, and able to think life a good thing" (Eugen was smiling to himself in great amusement), " I came to the conclusion that the best thing I could do was to leave the world."

" Were you going to starve yourself to death ? That is rather a tedious process, *nicht wahr ?*"

" Oh no ! I had not decided upon any means of effacing myself ; and it was really your arrival which brought on that fainting fit, for if you hadn't turned up when you did I should probably have thought of my interior some time before seven o'clock. But you came. Eugen, I wonder *what* sent you up to my room just at that very time, on that very day !"

" Von Francius," said Eugen tranquilly. " I had seen him, and he was very busy and referred me to you—that's all."

" Well—let us call it Von Francius."

" But what's the end of it ? Is that the whole story ?"

" I thought I might as well help you a bit," said I rather awkwardly. " You were not like other people, you see—it was the child, I think. I was as much amazed as

Karl, if I didn't show it so much, and after that ——"

" After that ?"

" Well. There was the child, you see, and things seemed quite different somehow. I've been very comfortable " (this was my way of putting it) " ever since, and I am curious to see what the boy will be like in a few years. Shall you make him into a musician too ?"

Courvoisier's brow clouded a little.

" I don't know," was all he said. Later, I learnt the reason of that " don't know."

" So it was no love affair," said Eugen again. " Then I have been wrong all the time. I quite fancied it was some girl ——"

" What *could* make you think so ?" I asked, with a whole-hearted laugh. " I tell you I don't know what it is to be in love. The other fellows are always in love. They are in a constant state of *Schwärmerei* about some girl or other. It goes in epidemics. They have not each a separate passion. The whole lot of them will go mad about one young woman. I can't understand it. I wish I could, for they seem to enjoy it so much."

"You heathen!" said he, but not in a very bantering tone.

"Why, Eugen, do you mean to say that *you* are so very susceptible? Oh, I beg your pardon," I added hastily, shocked and confused to find that I had been so nearly overstepping the boundary which I had always marked out for myself. And I stopped abruptly.

"That's like you, Friedhelm!" said he, in a tone which was in some way different from his usual one. "I never knew such a ridiculous, chivalrous, punctilious fellow as you are. Tell me something—did you never speculate about me?"

"Never impertinently, I assure you, Eugen," said I earnestly.

He laughed.

"*You* impertinent! That is amusing, I must say. But surely you have given me a thought now and then, have wondered whether I *had* a history, or sprang out of nothing?"

"Certainly, and wondered what your

story was; but I 'do not need to know it
to——"

" I understand. Well, but it is rather
difficult to say this to such an unsympathetic
person; you won't understand it. I *have*
been in love, Friedel."

" So I can suppose."

I waited for the corollary, "and been
loved in return," but it did not come. He
said, "And received as much regard in return as I deserved—perhaps more."

As I could not cordially assent to this
proposition, I remained silent.

After a pause he went on : " I am eight
and twenty, and have lived my life. The story
won't bear raking up now—perhaps never.
For a long time I went on my own way, and
was satisfied with it—blindly, inanely, densely
satisfied with it ; then all at once I was
brought to reason——" He laughed, not a
very pleasant laugh. " Brought to reason,"
he resumed, " but how ? By waking one
morning to find myself a spoiled man, and
spoiled by myself, too."

A pause, while I turned this information
over in my mind, and then said composedly,

"I don't quite believe in your being a spoiled man. Granted that you have made some fiasco—even a very bad one—what is to prevent your making a life again?"

"Ha, ha!" said he ungenially. "Things not dreamt of, Friedel, by your straightforward philosophy. One night I was, take it all in all, straight with the world and my destiny; the next night I was an outcast, and justly so. I don't complain. I have no right to complain."

Again he laughed.

"I once knew some one," said I, "who used to say that many a good man and many a great man was lost to the world simply because nothing interrupted the course of his prosperity."

"Don't suppose that I am an embryo hero of *any* description," said he bitterly. "I am merely, as I said, a spoiled man, brought to his senses, and with life before him to go through as best he may, and the knowledge that his own fault has brought him to what he is."

"But look here! If it is merely a question of name or money," I began.

" It is not merely that ; but suppose it were, what then ?"

" It lies with yourself. You may make a name either as a composer or performer— your head or your fingers will secure you money and fame."

" None the less should I be, as I said, a spoiled man," he said quietly. " I should be ashamed to come forward. It was I myself who sent myself and my prospects *Caput,** and for that sort obscurity is the best taste and the right sphere."

" But there's the boy," I suggested. " Let *him* have the advantage."

" Don't, don't !" he said suddenly, and wincing visibly, as if I had touched a raw spot. " No ; my one hope for him is that he may never be known as my son."

" But—but——"

" Poor little beggar ! I wonder what will become of him," he uttered, after a pause, during which I did not speak again.

Eugen puffed fitfully at his cigar, and at

* *Caput*—a German slang expression, with the general significance of the English "gone to smash," but also a hundred other and wider meanings, impossible to render in brief.

last, knocking the ash from it, and avoiding my eyes, he said in a low voice :

" I suppose sometime I must leave the boy."

" *Leave* him !" I echoed intelligently.

" When he grows a little older—before he is old enough to feel it very much, though, I must part from him. It will be better."

Another pause. No sign of emotion, no quiver of the lips, no groan, though the heart might be afaint. I sat speechless.

" I have not come to the conclusion lately. I've always known it," he went on, and spoke slowly. " I have known it—and have thought about it—so as to get accustomed to it—see ?"

I nodded.

" At that time—as you seem to have a fancy for the child—will you give an eye to him—sometimes, Friedel—that is, if you care enough for me—"

For a moment I did not speak. Then I said :

" You are quite sure the parting *must* take place ?"

He assented.

"When it does, will you give him to me—to my charge altogether ?"

"What do you mean ?"

"If he must lose one father, let me grow as like another to him as I can."

"Friedhelm——"

"On no other condition," said I. "I will *not* 'have an eye' to him occasionally. I will *not* let him go out alone amongst strangers, and give a look in upon him now and then."

Eugen had covered his face with his hands, but spoke not.

"I will have him with me altogether, or not at all," I finished, with a kind of jerk.

"Impossible !" said he, looking up with a pale face, and eyes full of anguish—the more intense in that he uttered not a word of it. "Impossible ! You are no relation—he has not a claim—there is not a reason—not the wildest reason for such a——"

"Yes, there is ; there is the reason that I won't have it otherwise," said I doggedly.

"It is fantastic, like your insane self," he

said, with a forced smile, which cut me, somehow, more than if he had groaned.

"Fantastic! I don't know what you mean.
What good would it be to me to see him
with strangers? I should only make myself
miserable with wishing to have him. I don't
know what you mean by fantastic."

He drew a long breath. "So be it, then,"
said he, at last. "And he need know nothing
about his father. I may even see him from
time to time without his knowing—see him
growing into a man like you, Friedel; it
would be worth the separation, even if one
had not to make a merit of necessity; yes,
well worth it."

"Like me? *Nee, mein Lieber;* he shall be
something rather better than I am, let us
hope," said I; "but there is time enough to
talk about it."

"Oh yes! In a year or two from now,"
said he, almost inaudibly. "The worst of it
is that in a case like this, the years go so fast,
so cursedly fast."

I could make no answer to this, and he
added, "Give me thy hand upon it,
Friedel."

I held out my hand. We had risen, and stood, looking steadfastly into each other's eyes.

"I wish I were—what I might have been —to pay you for this," he said hesitatingly, wringing my hand, and laying his left for a moment on my shoulder; then, without another word, went into his room, shutting the door after him.

I remained still—sadder, gladder than I had ever been before. Never had I so intensely felt the deep, eternal sorrow of life —that sorrow which can be avoided by none who rightly live; yet never had life towered before me so rich and so well worth living out, so capable of high exaltation, pure purpose, full satisfaction, and sufficient reward. My quarrel with existence was made up.

END OF VOL. I.

BILLING AND SONS, PRINTERS, GUILDFORD, SURREY.

S. & H.